Praise for *With Your Bad Self*

'A vivid and immersive story that speaks to the centre of human desire.'

—Jendella Benson, *Hope & Glory*

With a tone reminiscent of Nella Larson's *Quicksand*, *With Your Bad Self* leaves everything on the page; hope, regret and commitment to the choices we make, good or bad. A witty, heartfelt and sometimes gut-wrenching read from Fields—definitely a writer to watch.'

—Maame Blue, author of *Bad Love*

'A lyrical and beautifully composed exploration of love in all its complexity. The prose captures you from the start while the story keeps you reading until the very last word. Simply stunning.'

—Frances Mensah Williams,
author of *Strictly Friends*

Harkening back to literary greats like Ann Petry and Kristin Hunter, Kerika Fields's *With Your Bad Self* is an emotional knock-out. In Marie, we meet a woman whose desires were curtailed, but never killed, allowing us to interrogate the true natures of loss, liberation, and love. With an ear fine-tuned to the intricacies of language, and a compassionate heart calibrated to the many meanings of longing, Fields reminds us that life, though never perfect, can be a beautiful dance if we only allow ourselves to move with, and not against, it. I couldn't love this book more if I tried.

—Mateo Askaripour, author of *Black Buck*

With Your Bad Self

A Novella

Kerika Fields

JACARANDA

This edition first published in the United Kingdom 2023
Jacaranda Books Art Music Ltd
27 Old Gloucester Street,
London WC1N 3AX
www.jacarandabooksartmusic.co.uk

ISBN: 9781914344374
eISBN: 9781914344343

Cover Design: Rodney Dive
Typeset by: Kamillah Brandes

Photograph of the author on the jacket by Errol Fyfe/Hellen Collen Imaging

Cover photograph: Couple Dancing at the Savoy Ballroom, Harlem, 1947,
Bridgeman Images

MIX
Paper from
responsible sources
FSC® C018072
FSC
www.fsc.org

Dedication

I dedicate this book to those whose faces I can no longer look upon but whose voices I still hear and whose spirits are always with me.

My good, gone-to-soon sister friends Odette Blackwell and Judy Carn who always believed in my creative endeavors and laughed aloud at all of my jokes. You remain my light, ladies.

My forever friend Brook Stephenson, founder of the Rhode Island Writers Colony, for creating a safe space where I was able to write, hear my voice, and meet other wonderful writers. May we continue to carry your vision forward by any means necessary.

My father Rogers C. Fields for providing me with an excellent education at Epiphany and insisting all of your six children had a college degree. Not bad for a Black Boy from hard-time Mississippi.

My baby brother RasPinero Fields, a small seed that continues to grow in our hearts.

My cousins Ayofemi Richards, Robert Conner II, Cole Blaże, Mahmoud DeMattos, and Eugene 'Two Cent' McNeil for allowing me to experience your beauty and brilliance, however briefly.

My neighbour, Ms. Hattie Simmons, for the words of wisdom, constant prayers, parenting advice, and unbelievable belly laughs.

My Aunt Amy Tisdale for bringing me library books when I was a little Black girl in Brooklyn and for showing me what personal style looks like for real.

My paternal grandmother, Evelyn Fields, for providing me with my middle name, for giving me some great childhood memories, and for taking me to Cornerstone Baptist Church with you sometimes. Because sometimes, I needed it.

Mainly, I dedicate this book to my maternal Grandmother Marie Conner. Thank you for seeing me and loving me, contradictions and all. Thank you for teaching me how to cook—'cause, baby I can burn. And thank you for sharing your stories with me over the kitchen table down at Ashland; for remembering what you could the best you could. Because this is your story—truncated, reimagined, retold.

I tried my best to do you justice.

I pray I make you proud.

Chapter One

'This girl better be ready when I get there cause I ain't waitin',' Marie thought as she hurried up Fulton Street. She refused to be late for work this morning. Refused. This job was important to her. It allowed her to help her mother pay the rent on their fourth-floor Bedford Avenue walk-up. It also made it possible, finally, to help feed her eight siblings. Yes, sirree! This job ensured there was always something in the Frigidaire to eat. No more beggin' their stingy aunt who lived downstairs, who was also actually their landlord, for another goddamn thing. Marie could never forget the time, only a few years back, when they were all up there hungry as hell, and the smell from her aunt's place below of roasting chicken came wafting up into their apartment. But when her aunt, who knew they were hungry like everybody else was hungry during the damn Depression, came up to offer them some supper, the only thing in her pan was neck bones. Neck bones. The nerve. Just thinking about it made Marie's blood boil.

This job made it so she would never have to take a morsel of food from that woman or anyone else for that matter ever again. It also allowed her to buy herself some new shoes sometimes, which was a good thing because not only did she need shoes—this was New York City after all, and the weather changes, crumbling concrete, and constant walking tended to take its toll—but she loved herself some shoes, too. The shoes she had on this morning were black Mary Jane's with a low heel (but not too low!). She had just purchased them when she got paid that previous Friday from Abraham & Strauss. It was the following Friday now, she had been wearing them around the apartment all week after work while doing chores and cooking in order to 'break them in', and she was finally actually wearing them to work, even though she would have to change into the required white lace ups in her locker when she got there.

Turning the corner off Fulton Street onto Ashland Place, the shoes were still a little tight. She wiggled her toes, adjusted her back, held on harder to her shoulder bag, and kept right on stepping. As she approached the house, she hoped again that Missy was ready. She hated to have to wait. But she especially hated to have to talk to that old fool that owned the house where Missy rented her room.

Robert Conner had to be about thirty-three (which in her nineteen-year-old mind was actually ancient), and he lived alone there with his five-year-old daughter. Folks said he had been married and that his wife had died when the baby girl was just two, but Marie and Missy didn't know about any of that. All they knew was that Missy couldn't live with Marie, nor her own siblings and sick mother anymore, the rooms at Mr. Conner's were clean, affordable, and quiet, plus the house was conveniently located one block away from Brooklyn Hospital on DeKalb Avenue, where they both worked in the kitchen. So, when Missy turned eighteen she went on ahead and rented it. That was almost a year ago and so far, so good.

The heels of Marie's shoes clicked quickly against the concrete but slowed down the closer she got to 201 because Missy wasn't anywhere in sight. All she saw was him. But this morning, instead of hanging his big head out of the second-floor window saying stuff like, 'gal, stop yelling up to the window, will ya! It's too early for alla that!' or, 'you need to go on ahead and ring the bell like a lady. Why you making so much noise this mornin'? Your mama didn't teach you better?' he was sitting right there on the steps. And was that a smirk she saw on his face?

'Well, good morning, little lady,' Mr. Conner said deliberately not looking up or directly at her, acting like he was reading the morning's *Daily News*.

'Morning,' Marie mumbled. She was in no mood for mindless banter. Especially not with his tired ass. She knew good and well he was flirting with her. Even at her age, a girl knew these things. Her momma didn't raise no fool. Wasn't no other reason he made a fuss about her yelling up to the window. Horns beeping, people shouting, ambulances wailing, tires screeching all up and down the busy street, and all of a sudden, she was the noise problem? *Negro, please.* Silently, she sucked her teeth. She wanted to yell up to the window right then and there from the sidewalk the way she always did. But this time, she didn't. Something about the man's close proximity gave her pause. So instead, she stomped up the steps, right past where he sat, and rang the bell. Hard. Missy had better hurry.

'Making all that clickety clackety noise with them shoes. They must be new. Next time get the soft soles.'

Why wouldn't he shut up? And what gave him the right to comment on her shoes or her yelling or anything for that manner? That's why she hardly paid most men no never mind. They always thought they knew everything, thought they were smarter than women; when women and men alike knew good and well, that was not the case. Damn fools. She had brothers, so she knew. She had a good-for-nothing daddy that didn't even claim her as his own, too, so you *know* she knew. The way they talked loud about things they didn't know nuthin' about, the way they made messes they didn't clean up, the way they expected the world but didn't have a pot to piss in or a window to throw it out of. *Shiiit.*

She stood there for a minute, deciding what to do. Should she go on ahead to work or wait for her friend? Looking up at the

Williamsburg Bank clock, Marie realized she had only a few minutes to spare before she'd be late. Panicking, she forgot all admonishment, discarded all decorum, leaned back, opened her mouth, and yelled at the top of her lungs:

'MISSYY!!! I'm leavin'. If you ain't down here in one minute...'

Immediately Missy's head popped out of the third-floor window.

'I'll be right down. I'm coming right now!'

Marie could see that Missy's hair was done, and she had already put on her lipstick. Seemed her friend was ready after all, which reminded her... after reaching into her shoulder bag and fumbling around for it in the bottom of her purse, she pulled out her own lipstick. It had a small mirror on its imitation gold-plated case, which is what she liked best about it. Just as she was about to touch up her lips, Missy finally came on out the door.

'Let's go. I'm ready,' Missy said, clearly out of breath after running down them stairs. But since she had made Marie wait, Missy was gonna have to wait a hot minute, too. Marie looked into the mirror. One eye was on the clock behind her, its reflection hovering over her head, the clock you could see from Atlantic Avenue all the way to Myrtle and right on into Manhattan. The other eye was on her own full face. Sometimes doing something so simple as looking at herself in the mirror made her smile. She would never admit it to anyone aloud, but she knew it was true. She was beautiful. Smooth almond skin, plump lips, high cheekbones, head fulla hair. She acted like she didn't know but believe you me, she knew.

And Mr. Conner knew too. He could barely take his eyes off her. When they finally left the stoop, fast-stepping to work, even Missy, once she was sure her landlord was out of earshot, said so.

'Marie, I ain't never seen Mr. Conner look at nobody like he looks at you.'

'Well, I don't know what he's looking at. I ain't got no time for that old fool.'

'You the one being a fool!' Missy insisted.

Marie stopped mid-step and turned to stare at her friend. After a few silent seconds, she started stepping again. Hot on her heels, Missy kept talking.

'Mr. Conner a nice man. Got a house. Real friendly. Everybody in the neighbourhood knows 'im, and any woman ain't married from here to Ralph Avenue after him. And he only got eyes for you.'

'Well, good for him… just so long as he looks and doesn't touch! Besides…' Marie's voice trailed off.

'What? Besides what?'

Marie stopped again and, this time, let out a sigh. Momentarily her eyes glazed over.

'Girl, you know I'm crazy about that Benjamin. Can't stop thinking about him, hot damn!'

'He is a good-looking son of a gun,' Missy had to admit. 'It doesn't make no never mind, tho. Your momma ain't having you running up and down Fulton Street with that Negro, and you know it. He fine but…'

'Humph,' Marie thought to herself, 'my mother don't think nothing as black as Benjamin is fine, but she don't gotta know nothing.'

As they approached the hospital, other employees rushed into the building, pushing past them both, making Marie realize that if they didn't hurry, they'd be late to clock in. She was not about to let that happen. There was nothing she hated more than late Negroes, and she sure as hell was not about to be one, today or ever if she could help it.

'I'll talk to you about it later, girl!' Marie declared, dashing into the building. 'After work.'

'I'm doing a double shift tonight. Gonna have to catch you tomorrow,' Missy announced, rushing in her own right.

Marie ran up the stairs secretly glad that Missy couldn't see she was smiling. As much as she loved their ritual of coming to work together in the mornings and leaving with each other in the evenings, tonight, Benjamin was picking her up. She was relieved she was not going to have to explain their ever-evolving relationship to Missy, or worse, wonder if Missy would blab to her mother about who she was with or worse, run her mouth to her brothers. Marie had five of them, and they all thought they were in control of her life, even though she was the second to oldest sibling. Her brother Percy was just a few years older, but he acted like the man of the house, and since there *was* no man of the house, her mother let him go right on ahead acting like it. Ever since Marie had started filling out, working, making her own money, and leaving the house every day, he had a-hundred-and-one questions for her, *whatchadoinwhereyougoinwhyyouwearinthatwhattimeyoucominhome*?

And for some reason, even her younger brothers—William, who was called Bill because it was just easier to say; Charles, who they'd nicknamed Buster after that Buster Keaton from the pictures since he was always being silly; and Thomas also known as Midgie seeing that he was sorta stout and always would be—all felt they had a say about what she was up to, all except little Theodore, their Teddy bear, named after the former President, and who, at six, was too young to care.

Nobody needed to worry. Marie was mostly a good girl and was hardly ever up to no good, although she sure enough could not stop thinking about Benjamin all day. From the moment she clocked in, the *ch-chung* of her timecard going into the time clock puncher seemed to signal the countdown to when she would finally get to see her handsome Benjamin. He'd said something about a dance he wanted to take her to, and she couldn't wait. Not only was Benjamin tall and slim and black as molasses, but he was one of the best Lindy Hop dancers in Brooklyn. And coming from Marie Young, you ought to know that was saying somethin'. Yes, sirree! She was one of the best out there, no denying it. Even her big brother, Percy, had to admit it. After seeing her dance just last week at Mason's Ballroom, he said to her, 'go 'head with yo' bad self!' She loved him for that, for saying that to her. She knew it was just a street slang saying, the thing the kids on the block said to each other all the time, but she sure liked hearing those words thrown out there, especially if they were coming at her. They sounded like an affirmation, an acknowledgment. To her ears, those words sounded like love.

If you had on a new church outfit, you'd hear, 'go 'head with your bad self,' right before or after Sunday service; or if you got a new bike or even an old one for that matter, someone sitting on a stoop or hanging out of a window would yell out, 'go 'head with your bad self.' Everybody said it all the time where she came from. But coming from Percy, it really meant something. It made her feel good and just like when she started working at the hospital; real, real, proud.

When the hospital started recruiting again, most folks they knew applied for jobs there, even though hardly any of them got hired. Marie did, though, that's for sure. Everybody knew it was because her best friend, Missy, had put in a good word for her. That didn't matter none to her or to Percy either, and the night she told her momma and her brothers all about it, Percy, sure enough, smiled his big bright smile and said:

'Go 'head with your bad self, Marie.'

With the hospital job, she could help with the bills around the house, and it wouldn't have to be all on him, especially since it was looking like Momma's working days were behind her. Giving birth to little baby Amy three years ago had taken a lot out of her mother, Harriett, and it seemed to Marie like whatever it was that was gone, Harriett wasn't about to get it back anytime soon.

So, she went on to work. It wasn't an easy job, but if Missy could handle it, Marie sure could, too. Wasn't nothin' to it. Just peeling carrots and potatoes, chopping tons of onions, washing dishes and more dishes, and of course, scrubbing great big ole pots and pans that just seemed to keep coming. Even though Missy had been working there a year before she got hired to the hospital, Marie paid that no never mind. She was a quick study and got the hang of things real fast. It wasn't like this was her first job either. Seemed to Marie she'd been working ever since she could walk.

Back in Greensboro, North Carolina, before she and Percy come up to New York to be with Momma and her boys, Marie would help her grandfather catch and kill rabbits. The rabbits were fast, but little Marie was faster. She'd pull water from the well, too. And wash clothes in the bucket, then hang 'em on up on the line. One thing was for certain; Marie Young wasn't scared of no hard work. So, when Momma got pregnant and was too tired to take care of the babies she already had, it was Marie who changed the diapers, boiled the bottles, cured the colds, and quieted the crying. When her mother could no longer lift the mop bucket on account of her bad back, it was Marie who would sweep and then mop down the steps in that four-floor walk-up they were lucky to live in. If it didn't get done every single week, that meant the old landlord could charge her mother the full rent for their top-floor apartment, the whole twenty dollars a month. Lord knows they couldn't afford that. So she did what she had to do. That was one thing about that gal. If she saw something needed to be done, she went on ahead and did it, which was why she was gonna go on ahead and go to that dance with Benjamin tonight. She wasn't trying to stay out too late, anyway; she did have housework to tend to in the morning. She wasn't planning on doing anything foolish, either; she did have some sense. She just wanted to have fun, to finally feel young and free for a change. And for sure, she just wanted someone besides her big brother, Percy, to realize how bad she actually was.

As soon as she started thinking about the coming evening, Marie regretted letting her thoughts get away from her and not focusing her mind on the tasks at hand. Five o'clock wouldn't come soon enough. As she pulled her plastic protective bonnet over her hair, making sure not to mess up her freshly pressed and curled hair, she looked at the clock hanging on the wall, right there over the door, right there in her line of vision, and realized she had eight hours of workday left. It was only a quarter past nine. It was going to be a long day.

Chapter Two

At ten to five, Marie reluctantly went on into the ladies' room. She always avoided the workplace restroom if she could. It was crowded with co-workers and thick with all kinds of working-class woman funk. Most days, she'd wait until she got home to relieve herself, to finally freshen up in her own bathroom, which, even though it was shared with all her siblings and a sick mother, was always clean. She knew it was always clean because she was the one who always cleaned it. Today, though, there she was in the hospital's employee bathroom. After she'd finished up quickly in the stall, she went over to the row of sinks and washed her hands with the hard industrial soap that was put out for employees. It was the worst stuff, barely made any suds, and smelled like sulphur. But it was all she had at the moment, so she went on ahead and worked with it. After that, she dried her hands on towels that felt like sandpaper, shaking her head the whole time, wondering if it would kill them to put out some decent paper towels. Then she dug into her bag and pulled out her tube of lipstick.

She only owned three lipsticks altogether, but this was her favourite. The other two she'd brought from the five-and-dime drugstore on the corner of Fulton and St. James, where everybody bought almost everything. This one was from Duffy's, though. She rarely went to the high-end drug store further down Fulton Street just before just before you hit Brooklyn Heights, but the last time she did—running an errand picking something up for her landlord/aunt/rich bitch/evil witch—she decided that she wanted something for herself, too. She couldn't afford much; she hadn't started working at the hospital yet. The only money she ever got was some occasional change from the said landlord. It wasn't much, and mostly went to food for the house, the kids, her mother, cleaning supplies, toiletries, and the like.

That day she knew this day was coming, had blind hope that she would someday have reason to need that soft pink/beige silky lipstick in the silver tube that cost an unbelievable seventy-nine cents. Crazy, but Marie didn't care. She went on ahead and bought it. As she looked up into the unpolished mirror at work and applied it with a few smooth strokes to her full young lips, she was so glad she did. She looked good. The colour was subtle but noticeable. And that's what she wanted; to look good and feel pretty, not hot to trot, God-forbid.

The last thing she intended was to come off looking like Teresa Johnson, who was notorious for wearing too much mismatched makeup and was standing at the sink beside her, painting her coffee-coloured skin with a cinnamon-coloured face powder. It took away her hard-earned shine after a long workday all right, but it also made her look ashen, crusty, and confused as if she couldn't decide if she wanted to be light like the powder on her face or brown like the colour of her neck, ears, and hands. Poor thing. It wasn't Marie's place to say anything to her about any of that. Didn't the Bible say some-thin' somewhere about minding your own business anyway? Besides, she didn't care. All she cared about was looking pretty herself, for herself, and for her Benjamin.

'See ya tomorrow, Marie,' somebody said to her as she exited the broken-down bathroom, but she didn't know who it was. She didn't make eye contact or verbally respond, she just nodded and smiled, being sure not to smile too much or to let her happiness show. She'd learned not to share her God-given glow with just anybody. Most of the women that worked there were already jealous of her because she'd gotten the job so easy but were mainly jealous because she was an almond light, long-haired, natural beauty. They mistook her high cheekbones as an indication of haughtiness. She often overcompensated by being her down-to-earth self, always able to make the meanest mugs laugh and making any awkward individual entirely comfortable in her presence. But again, not today. Today she had other things on her mind, and that thing was waiting for her downstairs, right outside.

She rushed to clock out this time grateful for the *ch-chung* of her timecard going into the time clock puncher, releasing her out into the warm evening air. Before she knew it she saw ahead of her the familiar shoulders of the man she could not get out of her mind all damn day and flew toward him, and, still mindful enough to slow herself down a bit before he saw just how excited she was.

When he pulled her to him, and she kissed him quickly on his silky-smooth cheek, she was even more grateful for her lipstick choice. It had hardly smudged, which allowed her to walk beside him down the street away from the big hospital building towards the subway station they took to the ballroom without looking like she felt: excited, nervous, and a bit mussed.

It wasn't easy for him to play it kool, either. The casual talk, the catching up, the not touching, the hands hanging lank and loose on their sides simply said to the streets that they were just two young kids walking and talking in the atmosphere. Yeah. That's all anyone looking at 'em saw. What they didn't see was how Marie and Benjamin felt about one another, how they were on the same wavelength. He was as excited to see her, to even be near her, and she felt the same exact way about him.

Marie was grown enough to know that it didn't always go that way. She'd liked many boys who'd seen straight past her and had her own share of courters who couldn't understand she was just not interested and never would be.

But Benjamin.

When they finally got to the dance, he made sure to stand right behind her so that they could be close. Despite his six-foot three-inch frame towering over her five-foot four-inch own she could feel his heart beating as she shyly leaned against him while he removed her coat. They inched forward toward the ticket counter close like that and after he bought the tickets, he purchased two drinks and, leaning over, handed her an ice-cold bottle of Coca-Cola. It was simple stuff but all so subtle sweet sublime. The music played loudly and all the people were laughing and talking, but all she heard was Benjamin's heartbeat behind her. It was pulsing like an African drum sending sweet sensations all over her body. In an effort to suppress the scintillating sound, she gulped down her cold Coca Cola in one long swallow. She put the empty bottle on the table, placed one hand on her hip, tapped her foot to the live Bandstand's jumpy beat, and looked straight at Benjamin.

Marie was ready to dance.

One. Two. Three. They counted down to the beat together, and then, like firecrackers, they were off. Benjamin's warm hand held her steady and firm on her lower back, pressing perfectly, just enough to allow her to jump spin twirl without him ever losing touch of her.

The other kids were swinging, too: whoosh, around, up, over, under and then all of it all over again. But Marie barely noticed. To Marie, the other kids were background noise, irrelevant. She was the star of the this-here show, and this was her scene.

✳✳✳

The next day was Saturday, thank goodness. After finishing her usual household chores Marie had a little time to herself. Her mother was out at the doctor with Amy. As for her younger brothers… well, they could be anywhere. All they did was run around in the streets with their friends playing tag or stickball anyway. Most times she would pop her head out the window to see what they were up to, to make sure they weren't into too much trouble, to be sure they were doing all right. Today she didn't look out that window once. Let them fools run around the streets all day and all night for all she cared.

She was too busy basking in the memory of the previous night.

She remembered his hands on her waist, spinning her around the dance floor until all sense of time and space was lost. And his laugh. Oh God, he laughed so easily. At silly things and serious things, too. She couldn't help but laugh with him, which was a good thing since she could be way too worrisome, too serious, sometimes. She instinctively clutched her forehead when she suddenly remembered the kiss. Speaking of serious, hot dang, that was some kiss, right at the end of the night, right after she thought it would never happen, he just pulled her close and laid a real one on her! It wasn't no quick peck like the one she gave him when he picked her up after work, either.

This kiss was long and soft and sweet.

It was all she could think about all day until she realized that when he asked her out again, she had nothing to wear and, worse, wasn't no extra money to buy nothin' new. She started to sulk but quickly stopped herself, remembering instead to be grateful, to count her blessings. She had survived the Depression, damn near starved, and saw her siblings suffer right along with her. She'd witnessed her mother unable to find any kind of work and finally be able to get on relief. Now things were looking up. She had her job at the hospital, but she didn't make enough to be spending shit on fancy clothes and such. Luckily, her closet was full anyway. She had some nice things and she knew it.

When her mother did find work before she got sick, it was mostly cleaning white women's kitchens on the Upper East Side. Sometimes Harriett would come home with clothes for Marie from the women who no longer wore them due to weight gain or loss or simply because it was a new fashion season. Whatever the reason, the things were always in good condition, and Marie was happy to have them. She had some nice pedal pusher pants and a few knee-length pencil skirts, plus some silk blouses—some with buttons, some with bows, some with both. She'd also acquired a few lined wool skirts with well-placed pleats. Whatever she couldn't fit was altered so that it would. Her mother could sew pretty well, and so could Marie.

Along with her sewing skills, she was naturally stylish with a knack of knowing what to wear with what. She knew she shouldn't worry that she'd find something among the things she already had in her own closet for her next date, but Benjamin had been her friend for a while now, even before they started sneaking and dating, and she was convinced he'd seen her in everything she had already. For Marie, this would not do. She wanted to wear something different for Benjamin, something new. She wanted to look glamorous and sophisticated like Myrna Loy, or that there Greta Garbo, like the ladies in the picture shows who pursed their lips and batted their eyelashes and pretended to be all coy when they knew—along with everybody else except the guy—who was clearly in control. For Benjamin she needed something special. Just being with him made her feel like she was in a movie, like she was living a dream.

Her particular dream needed a specific wardrobe, and the next time she stopped by the house on Ashland to talk to Missy, it wasn't to pick her up for work. It was to put her to work. Well, not work exactly because that would imply that Missy was going to be paid for helping Marie make the perfect outfit and that sure enough was not the case. The case was: Missy could sew her behind off, even better than Marie or her mother, and she owed Marie a few favours. After all, Marie did beg and plead and finally convince her mother to let Missy stay with them, despite the lack of space, until she was eighteen and the city would leave her alone and let her be on her own.

Missy's own mother was a mess, always in the streets, drinking and carrying on with no never mind to her only child. Soon the city came knocking, demanding Missy produce a parent or guardian or else she would be placed in the system. That was almost two years ago and it had worked out fine for the most part despite the apartment's tight quarters due to all them boys. Harriett was reluctant at first, but she had to admit that Missy wasn't no trouble; wasn't one of those strutting up and down the street smoking cigarettes with grown men kind of girls. And of course, when she found out that the city gave out a little money for keeping her, Harriet said what the heck. Harriet had never wanted a foster kid, but this was Missy. She needed a place, and, well, Harriett needed the money. So, Missy moved on in, and the two girls became close, almost as close as sisters. Clearly, Missy could see right through Marie, her explanation for needing a new outfit as thin as the pattern paper they were cutting in front of them, but Missy didn't let on and let Marie go on with her made up reasons.

'You have some nice skirts in the closet at your momma's. Sure is silly to go to all this trouble to make a dress for a job you ain't even get yet,' Missy mentioned, trying not to make eye contact with Marie.

'Well, they say you have to dress for success. So I'm not tryna show up for the interview with some old hand-me-down skirt. Sure would be better to sport something sharp and new.'

Marie had told Missy that she was applying for a job at the department store downtown, even though they rarely hired coloured girls to work behind the counter, even though she already worked at the hospital. She'd said she could work there part-time and still keep her hospital job. Missy needed more convincing, so Marie poured it on thick.

'Besides, you're the best seamstress in Brooklyn. Used to sew alla time. Now every since you started working, you don't even bother with it no more. Figured I'd be your inspiration. See I can draw 'em, but I need your help sewing 'em.'

Marie held up a sketchpad where she had drawn a few dresses for herself. One with pleats, the other with a bulleted short side split.

'These are so good, Marie. You really shoulda went on ahead and applied to Pratt like your art teacher told you to. You got the eye for fashion, I tell ya gal!'

'Yeah, well, my art teacher told me to apply but didn't tell me how I was gonna afford the tuition or be able to eat while I was there. And she sure enough didn't tell me how to convince my mother that school was more important than workin'!' Marie's hands stopped moving on the scissors she was holding, and she sat for a spell, silent. 'That sure woulda been something,' she finally said.

'Going to that fancy college with all them cool cats, making things, learning new stuff every day…' Her voice trailed off.

Afraid melancholy would set in, Missy reminded her friend of something: even if she didn't go to no fancy college, she was still smart, and she was one of the most stylish girls in the neighbourhood. Those things you couldn't learn in nobody's college; you either had it or you didn't, and Marie had it in spades.

Marie was grateful for her friend's generous words and almost felt guilty for lying to her about the real reason she wanted a new outfit. But as the two girls finished cutting the pattern they'd drawn, and Missy began pinning it together, Marie could see it take its form, she could see herself in it, and best of all, she could see how Benjamin would love her in her new getup; he'd surely be smiling down with eyes all over her like he always did. So she didn't say anything about him to Missy; she didn't mention their date or that damn kiss. Instead, she smiled inside and kept her mouth shut.

There was once a time when she would tell Missy every little thing, wouldn't hardly make a decision before running it by her good friend first. That there was a while ago now, when they were just girls. They were becoming women, and Marie was discovering that part of being a woman was knowing what things to keep to yourself and what to share. Everybody didn't have to know everything all the time, she concluded, feeling sure enough grown-up at the realization.

Chapter Three

It was the fall of 1939 and everybody in Brooklyn could feel it. They could feel it in the cool menace coming from the muggy streets and, most notably, in the concern and confusion coming from each other.

The papers and radio stations screamed out the news: WWII had officially begun. When she'd heard the bulletin that morning, sitting there in the apartment with her mother at her side and little Amy asleep on her lap, the three of them huddled close to the old radio with its steady stream of static, Marie really didn't know what it all meant. Percy was off to work, and the boys were at school, which was a good thing since her mother had become visibly upset with the war announcement.

In her own naiveté, Marie couldn't see right then how what was going on over in Berlin and France and Germany could affect any of them. As far as she was concerned, she'd still be black and in Brooklyn. It was only until her mother sighed and said, 'now they gonna start that damn draftin',' did she realize what the war meant. Still, she did not completely know what to expect. She certainly didn't expect this:

'Marie, let's go on and get married.'

It was Benjamin who'd said these words to her only one week after the war had begun. She knew by then that boys, including her co-workers and her neighbours and her brother and soon her

Benjamin, were being drafted mighty quick, being sent off to fight in a war she still didn't (and never really ever would) quite understand.

She looked at Benjamin as she smiled broad inside, her heart at full swell. She wanted to hug him, to kiss him, to even finally have him, but all she could do was look at him. And blink. And blink. And blink some more.

'Girl, what's wrong with you?' her love demanded. 'Go on and say something already!'

Finally, with a million emotions in her heart and a million more questions in her head, she did.

'Well, yes,' she spoke, still dazed and confused. 'Yes, I'll marry you. I love you. You know I do.'

His question was a quick surprise, and so were his arms around her shoulders, his hands on her back, his lips on her face. All of him was suddenly all over her, hugging her, kissing her.

'But wait. Wait. First, you gotta ask my mother,' she said breathlessly, gasping for air, overwhelmed by his grabbing, hugging, holding as he'd never done before. She was a bit embarrassed, being alone with him like that right there in his own mother's apartment. She should have suspected something special might be going down when he asked her to come on up even though he never did; it just wasn't proper. Up until that point, she had never been alone with him. They were always, when together, surrounded by people; people on the streets or on the subway or on the bus or at the picture show or at the diner or at the dancehall. All the while it always felt like it was just the two of them, together, alone. And now they really were together alone and she wanted him so bad. His skin was smooth as silk, his black cheek was rubbing against her brown one while he stroked her thigh as he whispered in her ear.

'I love you. I always loved you.'

She immediately knew precisely what he meant. She'd always loved him too, ever since she caught him glaring at her in the high school auditorium at assembly, right there in a room full of teachers talking and students gossiping and giggling, amidst all the hushing and being hushed. They locked eyes, and she heard nothing at all anymore, but she sure did feel something. A warmth. A wanting. A curiosity. A connection. But this, this moment was different. So intimate. So intense. So sweet. Still... he had to stop, and she told him so, and so he did.

He pulled himself away from her warmth reluctantly with a slow sigh, his head hanging down in defeat. Her face was flush, her hair was a mess, and her skirt was scrunched up way past her knees. Marie felt a bit embarrassed for herself and didn't yet look over at Benjamin. She was afraid to see if he was mad or feeling frustrated. Instead, when he picked up his head and looked in her face, she saw he was smiling, so she smiled right back at 'im. Both of their faces shone bright as light bulbs. They just sat there grinning at each other until Marie noticed her skirt and snatched it down, quick, below her knees. Then they started giggling. Then they giggled some more. Then they just fell out laughing so hard they doubled over, slapping each other on the arm, the back, the leg. It was all so funny. It was all so lovely.

'Girl,' Benjamin said, exhausted and out of breath from nothing but laughter. 'You sho' are crazy.'

'I sho' am,' she replied without hesitation.

'And sassy, too. You sure is sassy, Miss Marie.'

'Sho am! Sure you can handle it, Mr. Soldier man?'

He looked at her again, looked at her grinning like that, and then grabbed her again into his long, strong arms.

'Long as I can hold on to you, I can handle anything.'

Chapter Four

'What? Wait! What do you mean she said 'no'?' The hurt on Marie's face hurt him so bad he had to look away.

'She just… well… your momma don't think we a good fit is all. She ain't giving us no blessing.' His head was down now, looking at his size thirteen feet as they slowly took the brownstone's steps, one by one. Soon he would be stepping in line—one, two, one, two—with other young, innocent men being sent to fight for their country. He would be away from her soon, unable to look at her across a room, to even just see her as she made her way toward him, or walked away. He knew this all too well, but still could not look at her now. He hated to lie to her, but he could not bring himself to tell his girl the truth, to reveal what Ms. Harriett had really told him, how she really felt. Instead, he feebly continued to insist to Marie that it was because he was going off to war and what kind of husband could he be, that he had no real money, no skills, and how would he take care of her, of them, and of his own ever-ailing mother, when he returned? He told Marie that her mother didn't think they knew each other well enough, that she didn't think they were ready. Tears ran down Marie's face as Benjamin spoke, as he told her anything he could think of, anything but what Ms. Harriett really thought of him, anything but the truth: that he was, according to her, 'too damn black!'

'I can't have my Marie running around town with a bunch of

little black babies. Look at you!' she'd said, bold as day. 'You damn near black as coal.' Then she had actually chuckled a little. At what he would never know and he did not ever want to know. The chuckle had a hint of mischief in it, of malice. The chuckle was meant to be mean.

'Now,' Ms. Harriett went on while standing up from her seat at her table and walking towards the kitchen sink, her back to him. She was preparing to wash the dishes. Clearly, Benjamin was being dismissed. 'You go on ahead, young man. Tell her. Tell her I said no. Y'all can't marry. She deserves better, and with her looks, she can get it.'

He backed up towards the door. He knew she wanted him to leave now, but he could not, not just yet. He had to tell the woman how he felt. He had to say it right out loud.

'But I love her, ma'am. I love her so much.'

There was that churlish chuckle of hers again.

'Your black ass don't know nuthin' about love. 'Cause if you did, you'd go on ahead and leave my child alone. Not try to burden her down with a bunch of black nappy-headed babies the world won't want. And where you gon' work, looking like that? Sure nuff not in no offices. White folks won't wanna look at you! They hate all niggers but 'specially the black ones. You'll hafta go on and workshop, witcha hands or something, and she the one gon' suffer. Marrying poor. She already poor. She ain't going from one poor house to the next one. I'll tell you that!'

Of course, he wanted to respond to her, to say more. He knew, though, that if he dared open his mouth again, whatever came out would be completely callous and definitely disrespectful. He would have to tell her she was so wrong and force her to look at her own self. Her light-skinned southern self. She, with all of her children from different fathers; she who'd never married. He'd have to tell her that she was simple-minded and colour struck and that even though she and all of her children were high yellow, they were all in the same place he and his blue-black mother was: broke in Brooklyn. They were all still struggling to make ends meet, to simply eat. Where were all her light-skinned lovers now, he'd have to demand of her. Yes, they'd given her those light, bright babies but nothing else.

Unlike Ms. Harriett, Benjamin was not a harsh person; he didn't have a mean bone in his body. He could never say these things to Marie's mother. Or to Marie, for that matter. So, when he got downstairs where Marie was waiting with painfully beautiful hope and optimism in her eyes, he did not tell her what her mother had said about him, did not tell her that her mother was an old fool and colourist and shamefully ignorant to boot. That Harriett was a racist in her own right and was too foolish to even know it. He didn't tell Marie he pitied her for having a mother who had taken the lies told to black southerners by their very oppressors and bought them with her up north—to The New York—where Negroes were finally free. He never mentioned his strange sense of relief of not having to deal with Harriet as a mother-in-law, as his family, forever. If her mother felt that way, he figured maybe Marie deep down felt these things about him, too? He should have asked for reassurance from Marie, or maybe he should have just gone ahead and said it:

'Your mother thinks I'm too black for you.'

Instead, he said:

'She thinks we are too young. You are not ready. My job doesn't pay enough. I still live with my mother.'

Marie opened her mouth to protest, but nothing came out. The tears streaming down her face said enough. How could you let her say no, she wanted to know, suddenly incensed by the sight of him. But then her ire turned towards Harriett. How could her mother deny her own daughter's happiness? Hadn't she been a good, self-sacrificing girl, a responsible, reliable daughter? She'd cleaned up her mother's messes and practically raised her illegitimate children, and now, when she had made her choice, her decision, her mother did not trust her enough to give her blessing, did not approve?

'To hell with her,' Marie finally spoke aloud. Although the words sounded good when she said them, they just didn't feel right in her soul. She would never wish hell on her mother, or worse, on herself by cursing the woman. Marie, ever blessed with wisdom far beyond her age, knew better.

'You don't mean that,' Benjamin confirmed. He knew Marie well. Normally this form of familiarity from him would warm her heart, this time, she felt nothing but the night breeze bring a curious chill to her bones. Benjamin felt it too. She could tell since he suddenly stuffed his hands into his pockets. Hands that should have been holding hers were now tucked away.

The sky was rosy, maybe even mauve, but not to those two, not that night. That night, all around and above them was as black and dismal as Ms. Harriet claimed Benjamin to be.

Benjamin began to walk away. Usually, he would make sure Marie was safe in her house before he turned to leave. But in her daze and disappointment, she realized she was walking him to the corner. He didn't discourage her. They were defeated, and they both knew it. Even though they legally didn't need permission to marry, Marie would never defy her mother, no matter what. The young woman was one who took to heart the sacred words, 'honour your father and your mother.' And since Marie had never met her father, having disgraced her mother back home down south to the point that Marie suspected it to be the one reason, among many obvious others, that Harriet was determined to leave. So to Marie, her mother, the only parent she had ever known, was sacred. She held Harriet's opinion and approval in the highest regard. Therefore Marie would not defy her mother; they both knew this was the stone-cold truth. So when they got to the end of the block, and she looked up at him, kissed him audaciously on the mouth right there in the street for anyone who was looking to see, then turned to walk back to her apartment, her mother, her brothers, her baby sister, her life, he didn't insist on escorting her, and he did not follow her. He just let her go.

That night, and countless days and nights thereafter, she cried. And cried. And since the apartment had only the two bedrooms to hold ten living souls, she had no privacy. Her heartbreak had earned her no solitude in which to sufficiently suffer. A few times, she tried to lock herself in their only bathroom, just sit there for a minute, think, feel, but she was always inevitably interrupted. So she stopped trying to hide her grief or stifle her sobs, or even quickly wipe away her hot tears when they came out of nowhere while washing the dishes or sweeping the floor or scrubbing the laundry on the washboard in the tub, then rinsing, wringing, hanging, and ironing all the clothes piece by piece. They would appear without warning, these hot thick unstoppable tears of hers. It was exhausting.

Her mother just looked at her, yet ignored her. Marie sensed that her mother was daring her to confront her, to ask why she'd said no, to demand an explanation, but she knew it wouldn't matter. Harriet had made up her mind, and for this, Marie was actually envious. Her mother was her own woman, able to make love, give love and get it from whom she chose or maybe whoever chose her, despite the consequences, the children, the abandonment. Marie did not understand her, but there they were, bound together, mother and daughter, two totally different people, always to be part of each other's world. Harriet's word was law in her world, so Marie avoided bringing Benjamin up altogether. She was too tired to talk any old way. All that crying was taking its toll.

Sometimes one of her little brothers would try to comfort her, would offer a kind word or attempt a hug (which she rejected, repulsed by any indication of intimacy), although they had no real idea what was going on with her. They assumed it was because of Percy—who had been drafted a few weeks earlier. Even though, of course, she missed her big brother, even his control issues and constant meddling, that was not it. That was not the source of the uncontrollable tears, the unbearable pain. No, her siblings did not know her heartbreak. Her mother definitely did, though, yet offered no comfort, no words of salve, no support. Instead, she made sure to keep Marie busy, with the cooking and the clothes washing and the caretaking.

Marie was used to this kind of work, especially being the oldest daughter and the only daughter for so many years until young Amy was born. Still, it seemed like ever since her mother had destroyed her dreams of marrying Benjamin, the workload was heavier. Grimy. Tedious. Monotonous. Was this to be her life? Was this it for her? Cleaning her mother's apartment? Tending to her mother's many children? This here was her mother's life. Her mother had created this situation, and Marie was just born into it and seemed to be stuck right the hell in the shit. And she was pissed. Didn't she deserve her own type of love? Her own life? Nice things? To dance? To meet interesting, smart, creative people? To travel? To wear fine fashions?

Once bubbly, funny, sometimes sweet, and often optimistic, Marie was now—basically—bitter. Heavy-hearted and disappointed, the bright light behind her eyes had been reduced to a flicker. It was a doggone shame, too, since that Marie was one girl who always had a pep in her step. Goddammit, she coulda been a derby girl skating and pummelling her opponents as she did two summers ago, until Percy said stop, told her good girls didn't bash on each other, compete, fight, sweat, speed around, win. Nowadays, she stomped to work and slid on home. People passed her on the street, those who knew her said, 'hey, how ya doin' Marie?' and she always answered, 'fine.' But she wasn't nearly fine. And no one seemed to care or even notice except Mr. Conner.

As usual, he was sitting on the steps when she showed up in the morning to fetch her friend for work. And as usual, Marie wished he wasn't there; she did not want to be bothered. Nevertheless, she was never really outright rude to the man, and despite her smart-ass, sassy responses to his annoying questions and comments, she usually managed to keep her composure.

Not this day, though. This day, since she was disgusted with the whole wide world—why, was there a stupid war? Didn't she just survive the Depression? Why didn't her mother approve of Benjamin?—you know good, and well, she was disgusted with him and his self-righteousness, sitting there, grinning like a Cheshire cat, as if he knew her, like he knew anything at all about her. Old arrogant ass.

As she started up the steps that day, she knew for sure he'd better not say anything smart to her, or else she would not be responsible for what came out of her mouth that morning. But, of course, he could not help it. So, of course, neither could she.

'Ahh, there she is.'

It was seven forty-five in the morning, yet there he was, up and awake and sitting smugly on the steps reading the newspaper. It was his house, after all, so he sure could do whatever the hell he wanted to do, Marie reasoned in her head, but why couldn't he just grab the morning paper and take it on into the house to read over a cup of coffee in his own kitchen or something, like a normal person?

'Hey. Mornin',' she mumbled, wishing he would go away already, wishing for the chill of winter which might effectively keep his ass in the house. She just wanted to get her friend, get to work on time, get through the damn day and get the hell on home. At nineteen years old, at that moment, that was all she wanted out of life.

'Well, what's stuck in your claw this fine mornin' Miss Marie?' he said because, to Marie's disdain, he had to say something. He simply could not *not* say anything to her, for once. No sirree.

She took a deep breath, stepped past him, and pushed the bell. She had already said good morning, and that wasn't even easy.

He clearly wasn't going to make it any easier.

'Not speaking today, huh?' His words were caring and full of curiosity, but she only heard condemnation.

'Look, man. I done said good morning. Now what the hell else you want me to say?'

Her finger was hard on the bell, and within a few seconds, Missy's head was out of the window.

'I'm coooming!'

'Well, come on then! Why I gotta wait for you every morning? I don't know why it's so hard for you to be ready when I get here,' Marie barked back before she turned her wrath towards poor Mr. Conner.

'And why every morning you sitting here, smiling, trying to talk me up like you know me? You don't know me! You don't know nothin' about me, mister.'

He closed the newspaper, its headlines screaming of more war attacks in Europe, news that always inevitably made her sick to her stomach these days. But he didn't notice her nauseated look; he was too busy admiring her firm figure. She sure was a pretty little thing.

'Well, I guess I owe you an apology for trying to be nice. Because you know what? You're right. I don't know you. Not at all. But maybe we can change all of that.'

'What's that supposed to mean?' she asked half-heartedly. She was not looking at him at all but was instead staring aimlessly up at the Williamsburg clock again, wondering when the almost always late Missy would come on already, figuring that between her slow friend and this old fool, she might be better off going straight to work in the mornings from now on. Missy could get to work on her own. What the hell were they, anyway? The Bobbsey Twins? Her recent relationship fail had suddenly made her feel very grown-up, mature, independent, and alone. She didn't need anybody, and she surely didn't need this shit.

'You know what I mean, girl. Come on out with me.' He laid the newspaper down beside him now and stood up. They were eye to eye, almost, due to the mere two inches he had over her five-foot, four-inch frame. 'Come on,' he continued. 'I'll take you uptown to Wells'. It'll be fun. You look like you need some fun.'

'I need a lot of things, Mr. Conner, but fun ain't one of 'em.'

'You sure about that?'

'Yeah, I'm sure.' She managed a slight smile, but really she wanted to spit. Plah. Right there. Right in front of him. Right on his own steps. As soon as she thought it, she actually felt her mouth water, her cheeks gathering saliva in preparation, and she was disgusted with herself. Who in the world was she? Who had she become? Why was she allowing Benjamin's rejection and her mother's betrayal to make her, well, mean? Mean enough to spit! She hated mean people. Surely she did not want to hate herself. She'd survived the worst without becoming mean. She'd been hungry, tired, cold, and mad. But never mean. Never spitting mean. She'd stood on her share of long lines, being sure to be right there at Brown Memorial Church at dawn on Thursdays so she would get some of whatever they had to offer that week—some bread, some flour, some rice, some powdered milk something being better than nothing—and it never made her actually angry.

Yet, here she was, mad as hell at a man. And her own mother. And she didn't like herself like that. She wanted to be happy. She needed to be treated nice. She deserved to dance, to fix herself up, to go on out. Have a laugh. Share a smile. Sip a drink. She needed to not be mean anymore. So she looked right back at the old man and said straight to his face:

'Oh, what the hell.'

Chapter Five

One thing about that Robert Conner: he sure was a sharp dresser. When Marie saw him standing outside her building in a brimmed bowler hat, well-tailored double-breasted suit with a paisley pocket square, and sure enough shined up buckskin shoes, she almost forgot he was short. But she didn't forget not to act like she noticed. She had no intention of letting him know he'd impressed her already, so early in the evening. As far as she was concerned, he had a lot more impressing to do, and it was gonna take more than some fancy duds to get her ship sailing. Especially since she wasn't slouching herself.

In anticipation that he would take her somewhere sophisticated and mature, she stepped out looking sharper than Hazel Scott on a Sunday morning. Marie wore a knee-length wool pencil skirt in slate grey with pearled buttons at the hip that ran up the side and a fitted black satin jacket with a wide lapel that nipped her right at her slim waist. On her head, a small pillbox hat sat pinned atop a mound of freshly pressed curls. A small veil peeking out from under it slightly covered her right eye. The mesh veil had little polka dots all over it, which matched the polka dots in her sheer black pantyhose. Her shoes that evening? The same Mary Jane's she'd worn the morning her date had accused her of making too much noise by walking up the block. She wondered if he'd say anything about them tonight. But, as she gripped her herringbone-handled handbag, she realized she did not care. She still missed Benjamin. All this was just a distraction, something for her to do with herself besides think about him. That's right. She thought about his black ass every Goddamn day. How was he doing over there? Was he holding up all right? Was he flying planes or sailing on the ships or cooking or fighting? She had no way of knowing. All she really wanted to know, though, was, did he miss her? Did he think about her, too? She constantly wondered about what could have been between them. Did he regret not fighting for her, for their love, for their future together? So many questions she didn't want to ask and feelings she didn't want to feel, not one more minute.

So she listened when Robert (or Bob as he insisted she call him) talked about his work as a head electrician right down there at the Brooklyn Navy Yard not too far from his house or the hospital. He told her he'd served in WWI in Europe and nearly died delivering messages between base camps, a dangerous job that no one wanted, but since he was a Negro soldier and a smart, sturdy one too, he was given the honours. She found out that night that when he got back from the war, he went on to school at that there Howard University in Washington D.C. with all them other bougie Negroes. No wonder he thought he knew every damn thing, she thought to herself. But Marie did not bother to say any of this. To do so would have meant she actually wanted to engage, that she actually cared, which she did not. So she just smiled, looked pretty, and let him talk all about himself all night.

As she simply listened, she also learned that that house he owned used to be his mother's who bought it when the white owners died with the wages she'd earned and saved while cleaning it most of her life. Marie had to admit she'd wondered about how a single black man got ahold of such a nice piece of property. Oh, sure, there were black people that owned homes, but they were mainly business people or doctors or lawyers and such. Even still, it was nothing like with the

Italians and the Jews who owned buildings and businesses and hired their own to keep the money in their families and communities. From what Marie could see, black folks still seemed to be waiting for the Forty Acres and a Mule they were promised way back when before they really got going on their own.

Most in the city were from the South, having come on up with the Great Migration, former slaves with no real schoolin' or skills 'cept for cooking and cleaning and building and such, so this Mr. Conner here was sure something else. A few, with any gumption and imagination, managed to make good money their own way, as did her beloved Aunt Ida and her restaurant, with her bad self. Marie sure didn't want to dwell on the mysterious disappearance and current whereabouts of her favourite Aunt that evening, either, so she bopped her head as the music played and sipped slowly when the champagne cocktails arrived.

Mr. Conner had taken her all the way to Uptown. To Wells'. Hot Damn. None of her friends had been to any of those famed nightclubs in Harlem. No way. They were still running around with Brooklyn boys. Roller skating. Lindy Hopping. Sharing sodas. Sneaking beer. Puffing Bogies. They could keep that shit from now on as far as Marie was concerned. She did all that and then some with Benjamin—it was fun, she had to admit—but he'd left her behind, and she was leaving all that foolishness behind her for sure. From now on, it was cocktail dresses and fancy parties and frosted champagne glasses for her. From now on, she was going to live, her mother, her brothers, whoever, be damned. She wasn't sure how but she was going to have herself some excitement, some adventures. She wasn't going to live the rest of her life in Brooklyn as her mother seemed doomed to. She was going to find a way, she just didn't know how.

The next morning the answer to Marie's wanderlust was right there in the day's paper. There they were, good ole' Government Job Openings. 'Young American women are needed as Secretaries,

Stenographers, Phone Centre Attendants, and Office Assistants. Apply now. Must be willing to relocate.'

She stared at the paper in somewhat disbelief. After her night out with Mr. Conner, after he'd made her laugh a few times, after he introduced her around to his stuffy assed old friends, after he'd rubbed her leg all up under the table all night, after she'd let him give her a wet Bourbon-infused uninspired non-Benjamin kiss good-night in his car, after her mother and brothers had left the house that morning she was so excited that she dressed up the baby, put her in the carriage, and went to see if Missy had seen the announcement, too. Mama had gone food shopping and had left baby, Amy, there with her to watch for God knew how long. But Marie really didn't' mind. That Amy was one sweet baby; nice and quiet and thoughtful. Easy. Not like them damn boys jumping up and down and yelling all the time for no reason at all except they were boys, and that's what boys did.

She'd waited 'til almost noon to go see Missy, since it was their day off from the hospital, and she wanted to let her friend sleep in like she damn well deserved. Plus, she didn't want to run into Mr. Conner that morning. Didn't want to get him to thinking she was on pins and needles waiting to see him again cause that was not the case. And after that drunk, sloppy kiss he laid on her, she didn't want to embarrass him, either. He had to be ashamed, and if he wasn't, she was shamed enough for him: a grown-ass man not even smooth enough to sweep her off her feet when presented with a God-given opportunity, one he sure 'nuff wasn't gonna get again.

Walking down Fulton Street, her head was full of ideas, of ways she could live not if, but when, she got herself one of them Government Jobs. The things she could buy. The things she could do! She imagined having lunch all by her lonesome, not having to share nothin', and paying the bill her own damn self. Yes, of course, she would send money home to help her momma, but she'd save most of it, after she did a little shopping and made sure she looked good with some of them nice skirts and fitted jackets. Store-bought, not handmade. Brand new smelling like the store, not hand-me-downs smelling like some rich white lady's perfumed cigarette smoke. She was gonna have it made in the shade, that's for sure.

She wondered what it would be like, to live in another city like Washington there. She loved Brooklyn no doubt; it wasn't nothing like the people and the parties. But Brooklyn wasn't the world, and she wanted to see maybe not all of it but at least some of it. This job would be the beginning of her adventures. She was so filled with anticipation of a new life that she was literally shaking, thinking of them fresh opportunities. Besides, all Brooklyn did nowadays was remind her of Benjamin. Everywhere she looked—the corner store, the subway station, the park, her stoop—she saw his fine black ass standing around smiling somewhere. She couldn't shake the images of him, which made her so sad and mad that she made her own self sick. Yeah, she thought, as she rounded the corner off of Fulton Street and onto Ashland Place, being sure to manoeuvre the rickety second-hand stroller deftly so that Amy was not disturbed. Yeah, this is it, baby. I'm applying. I'm going, and I'm a talk Missy into going with me. With our work experience at the hospital, we are a shoo-in. We gonna get them jobs, then we gonna go on ahead and set that city on fire. Hot Damn!

Chapter Six

She wanted to burn her oldest brother with his own cigarette. Standing there smoking in their momma's house even though she never let anybody smoke inside. But Percy wasn't anybody; he was Harriett's firstborn, a boy, and her forever favourite. So there he stood with his stupid self and his stinky cigarette, telling Marie what she could and could not do. Her bigheaded brother, not even the war wanted 'im.

When she got in from visiting Missy—who was not at all interested in applying to the job notice—there he was. Flat-footed fool. Seems he was discharged from service about a week ago and—just her luck!—had arrived home the very day Marie needed her mother's ear all to herself. But who was she kidding? Even if her big brother wasn't back home her mother probably would not have approved of her applying. But at least Harriett was her mother. Who the hell was he—her brother, not her father, not a parent—to tell her what she could and couldn't do?

Well, according to Percy, no single sister of his was going off to a job in another state all by her lonesome. It just wasn't right, Percy said, and her mother agreed. They loved her, they both insisted, and would never let her make such a huge mistake. What would happen if she needed them? If she got hurt? How would they help her if she was attacked, robbed, accosted, or preyed upon by strange men because of her innocence, her youth, her blackness, her beauty? It wouldn't look right, a young single girl living in a new city all alone.

As Percy persisted in projecting his opinions onto her life, all Marie heard was fear. Scared niggas always trying to stop somebody else from breaking free. Did they expect her to just sit up there in that apartment for the rest of her life? That would surely work for her mother; Harriett would have someone to tend to her home, to help her care for all her children. It would work for Percy, too. Give him someone to watch over, to control, 'cause them Brooklyn bitches he ran with in the streets was all about their business, and his broke ass couldn't do nothin' for none of 'em and he knew it.

Marie was pissed and wanted to tell the both of them to kiss her ass, but she couldn't. Mainly, it wasn't in her nature. She could curse anybody out with the quickness, no doubt about it, but not her mother. Never her own mother. Besides—all love and approval aside—she actually needed both of them right then to help her pay for the application already. It was only two dollars, and the deadline was that day. She'd have to go to the post office and get a money order to mail it on out in time, but she didn't have the money right then, having had paid her mother's rent and buying food for the house with her last paycheck. She couldn't believe it her own self and cursed her insistent inability to always put some change aside. But it wasn't always that easy. There was always something coming up. And since she was working and most weren't, someone was always coming to her for something. Someone needed a jacket for the winter or some books for school. And when she had it, she gave it; that's the kind of girl she was, was always the kind of person she wanted to be. Nobody should ever want for nothing if she had a hand in it, as far as she was concerned. If her mother or her brothers or her friend or even her neighbour needed something, they knew they could come to Marie. Everybody knew straight up that if she had it—time, energy, an ear, a little extra money—she'd share it for sure. But sure enough, when she needed something, nobody came up offa nothin'. Nobody had nothin' to spare. And sure enough, that's what Percy told her: he didn't have no money. He just got back in town, he reminded her. And her mother had a sob story too, even though Marie knew her Harriett always kept some spare change in the house somewhere, or at least she imagined she did, 'cause how the hell you gonna have all these kids and not have some kinda stash somewhere, at least to be able to get 'em something in a pinch? But according to her mother and her older brother, they simply didn't have it. They couldn't help her.

Marie looked at the both of 'em with eyes that knew their *couldn't* really was a *wouldn't*. She knew them Negroes was so selfish and scared that they wouldn't give her the two damn dollars it would take to send on in with her job application. They knew that if they didn't help her right then and there she'd miss the deadline and wouldn't even be able to apply. And everybody was applying. All the young women. From everywhere. From all over the country. 'Specially from there in New York. That's why she couldn't even go to any of her girl-friends to borrow a couple of bucks. Two dollars was a lot of money, and nobody had it, and if they did, they weren't coming up off it 'cause they never knew when or how they would see it again. But her brother? Her mother?

For a moment, she was tempted to stay and wait until the apart-ment was empty and look through her mother's things, find the stash she knew she had to have hidden somewhere in there and grab them two dollars she needed for the job application outta sheer spite. But one thing Marie knew about herself was that she wasn't a damn thief. Any fool that would steal from their own momma deserved all the bad luck life could give 'em. So she shook off that sinful thought and instead mumbled 'these mother fuckers' to herself, over and over again in her head as she stood up, and, as if in a trance, walked out of the apartment, down the stairs she'd swept, past the stoop where she'd seen Benjamin that last time, and across the street from where she'd arrived at age five from North Carolina with just a sandwich in a sack to finally be with her mother.

Harriet had left her and Percy down south in North Carolina with her Grandpa Youngblood (yes that was indeed the old Indian's original name. He ended up dropping the 'blood' when he was just a boy so he could get work and some respect and such, leaving his family with the name Young, since down south the only thing them crackers hated worse than a Negro was a Native American) until she got her stuff together and could send for them for good.

Back then, to Marie, the North seemed so new, so exciting. Of course, it did—she was just a little six-year-old girl coming from the South to the new big city. But the shit was old now. And Marie was tired. City life was totally tiring. At least in the country you could grow your own food, run on down to the river to quench your thirst with freshwater, catch and skin a rabbit just like her grandfather taught her if you didn't have anything else, or plain pick an apple off a tree in a pinch. Here, to eat, you had to hustle. Everything was a hustle.

She kept on stepping—mad and hurt and confused—the sounds of the streets a blessing in her ears, allowing her not to hear her own voice screaming inside her head, the chaos of the city streets literally giving her life. The music and the madness and the laughter and the beeping car horns and the babies crying and the corner boys cursing and the girls giggling right along with the police sirens wailing put her on autopilot, allowed her to just step on, to keep movin', to walk. One foot in front of the other was all she knew right then. She didn't even know where she was going, but she knew she didn't want to go back home to her mother's. She desperately wished she had another place, her own place, sorta like the one she coulda had if she'd gotten that government job.

Suddenly, she found herself missing her Aunt Ida real bad. She'd surely had given Marie the money for the application. Woulda told her to go ahead with her bad self, get that job, make that move. 'Cause Aunt Ida was a woman about her business who always had money in her pockets and change to spare. If there was a way to make a decent dollar, Aunt Ida knew what it was and when she opened her restaurant couldn't nobody tell her nothin'.

It was a small joint with only eight tables but it was her pride and joy. She may have been Harriett's little sister, but she was the big girl of the family. Owning up, thinking, planning, creating solutions, not waiting around for government handouts, and for sure not having a whole bunch of babies no one could afford to feed. That's why she always had time for Marie, who she called her 'favourite niece' (even though, at the time, Marie was Ida's only niece), to anyone who would listen. So when she opened her little diner, suitably simply named Ida's, right there over on Herkimer Street, she insisted Marie help her out by greeting guests, serving plates, clearing off tables, and wiping up spills and such.

At first, Harriett said no. She didn't want her daughter out and about serving grown folks. But once Ida told her she'd pay Marie, let her keep her tips, and allow her niece to bring home food when there was any left? Well, what could Harriett say? She had to admit Marie was a young woman who needed things she couldn't get her, and surely Ida needed someone who could work hard and who she could trust. So Harriett gave Marie permission to work at the restaurant after school and one day on the weekend. Marie chose Sunday even though she knew that was the Lord's Day—a day reserved for church and rest. But she also knew that was the day when people went out to eat right after church for Sunday Brunch or were ready to grab breakfast real early in the morning after a night of hard partying Saturday night. Hung-over and hungry, they were sure to go somewhere to get some fresh fried eggs and good grits with sizzling bacon or ham or some fluffy pancakes with syrup thick as molasses served with coffee hot like fire. Ida's place was the spot, and sure 'nuff Sundays were the days Marie made off with the most tips. People sure are generous on the Lord's Day.

Marie sighed right there in the street. Those were the good old days, she thought to herself, even though it was only two years ago. Two years since she stopped working for Aunt Ida, two years since she last saw her Aunt. Her heart hurt remembering it all. Remembering the day she went to the restaurant and it was closed down with Aunt Ida standing there in the foyer looking hurt, a little scared, somewhat stressed, but somehow still strong.

Marie would never forget what her aunt said and how she said it. With her only good suitcase in one hand and a lit Lucy Strike in the other, Aunt Ida looked straight at Marie and made it plain as day:

'Girl, I gotta go.'

Marie's heart immediately began to race, her mind full of questions.

'Go where Aunt Ida? Ida, where you going?' All efforts to be nonchalant about this disturbing news were absolutely pointless since Marie heard the confusion and desperation in her head come right on out with the words from her mouth. Ida heard it too. She looked at her niece, said nothing, and took a long drag on her cigarette.

Marie had more questions. 'And what about the shop. Why we closed today? You need me to start preppin' the place?'

'Listen, baby. You don't need to worry about any of that,' Ida assured her, breaking her smoke-filled silence. 'Now. Like I said. I gotta go. And I'm leaving soon. Today. Getting' right on the train that leaves at noon. Got a few extra things to take care of then I got to go.'

Marie felt her eyes begin to burn with the threat of tears, but she didn't dare let one teardrop fall down her face. If it was one thing she knew her Aunt Ida didn't have time for, it was tears. So she swallowed hard and said:

'You scaring me.'

Aunt Ida laughed a little, stamped her cigarette into the ashtray, and waved away the smoke along with Marie's words of worry.

'Girl ain't nothing to be scared of. Just listen. Like I done said. I'm leaving come noon. And I ain't going to be back most probably. Now, you are welcome to come on with me. Everything's gonna be alright.'

Marie's mind began racing all over again, this time with excitement. Aunt Ida was leaving and she was going with her. To where she didn't know, but she knew it'd for sure be an adventure. Her Aunt was always on to something and could surely survive anywhere she decided to go. She'd survived the South. She'd survived Brooklyn. She'd be just fine wherever else she was going, that was for sure. Ida had the gift of gab, was smart and stylish, and was always about her money. She had friends everywhere, could relate to everybody, and was able talk to anybody about anything. Not bad looking either. Pretty pecan-coloured face with high cheekbones and full lips; deep dancing dark brown eyes; big round behind. Yeah, her Aunt Ida was gonna be all right, Marie knew. And she'd...

'But listen, baby,' Ida interrupted her thoughts. 'You can come on with me, but if you do, you can't be in touch with your momma and them no more. I got to be clear on that.'

'What? Why not?'

'You just can't.'

Ida grabbed her purse off the counter and picked up the small suitcase that sat by her feet.

'I ain't got time to be answering no whole heap of questions. Now I done told you what I could tell you. If you coming, come on. If not, that's ok too.'

She grabbed Marie by the shoulders, hugged her real tight real quick, and then walked on out the door.

Marie stood there in shock. The restaurant, which was usually bustling with business that time of day, was quiet as a cathedral. All she could hear was the ticking of the clock. She looked up at it there on the wall over the counter and realized it was a quarter to eleven in the morning. Around this time, they'd usually be getting ready for the lunch crowd, wiping tables, filling water pitchers, and checking the cash register for change. But not that day. Not anymore.

After a few moments, Marie knew she had to get moving. But she wasn't sure what she was going to do. Was she gonna go on ahead with Aunt Ida or stay at home with her mother, where she supposed belonged? Her mother needed her. She couldn't just up and leave her, could she? Wouldn't Marie miss her and her siblings eventually? And what was that about not being able to keep in touch? Clearly, Aunt Ida was running from something or somebody. Her mother would worry herself sick. Marie thought hard about it but decided that running just wasn't right; it just wasn't fair to nobody. So she sighed and decided she wouldn't go.

So she got on out of the restaurant and went on home. But soon as she got there, back to that crowded but clean apartment, she knew she wanted to be gone. She knew she wanted to be free. Looking around the place all alone while her brothers were at work and at school, while her mother was out picking up her relief check for the month, Marie knew it was the quiet before the storm; she knew that as soon as Harriett got home she'd tell her to cook whatever she'd brought in from the market. Then she'd be washing dishes and scrubbing pots. Then them boys would be in the living room there knocking things all over the place, making a holy mess that Marie would inevitably have to clean up.

She knew she didn't have the stomach for it anymore, for her mother, for her mother's mess, for her mother's children. And then, suddenly, she had gone and done it, the one thing every woman had the right to do whenever she pleased: she'd changed her mind. Just like that, in a split second. Looking at the clock in the kitchen, she saw she still had a little time but not much. Marie decided to go for it. She wanted to leave her mother a little money until she realized she didn't have any; she hadn't made any tips from Ida's that day. So she threw her things into a big bag quickly, used the powder room real quick, and ran on out the door, down the steps, and into the summer street.

It was one of those hot and humid-as-hell days, and no, there was no breeze. She tried walking fast, but the heat coming up from the concrete on the sidewalks and the asphalt in the streets seemed to be pushing against her, slowing her down. She could see the waves of heat rising up right in front of her. It didn't help none that her saddlebag was so heavy. She'd stuffed everything she could into it but was wishing she had left some things behind. But she didn't stop. She was sweating bullets, but she kept stepping as fast as her feet and the heat would allow.

Soon as she hit Fulton Street and Nostrand Avenue, she knew she was too late. The L train, which she'd watched being built years earlier, was pulling right off, right in front of her face. Any other day she woulda had to wait ten minutes for it, any other day the damn train woulda been late. But not that day. That day the Fulton L train was right on time, speeding away from her with her Aunt Ida along for the ride. Right then Marie couldn't swallow her tears, couldn't hold 'em back, couldn't imagine a time when there would be so much pain and disappointment heavy in her chest, bringing her down. She stood there in the street staring up at the receding train and cried until her tears soaked the front of her shirt. Thankfully it looked like sweat to strangers, but she knew better; she knew the stain was a result of a frustration she'd never experienced up to that point.

But that was before Benjamin and before today when she felt so alone, so despondent, so unsupported. That was before she had become so world-weary that her heart physically hurt. What was the point of wanting shit when it seemed like you never could get it?

She wanted to sit on some stranger's stoop; she just wanted to stop right there in the street. Now that she had conjured up memories of her favourite aunt she was suddenly emotionally exhausted and all she wanted to do was sleep. Sometimes she dreamt of Aunt Ida and could see her clear as day, just a-laughing and looking sharp as a tack, as usual. Most days, in her waking hours, Marie tried not to think about Aunt Ida because remembering filled her with regret: she shoulda went on with her when she had the chance. She shoulda been more decisive. She shoulda been more sure of herself.

If she had been confident and brave, she wouldn't be stuck now, looking to her mother and her oldest brother for their opinions on what she should do with her own life. 'You only get one life, so you might as well do what you want to do,' is something Aunt Ida would wisely say. Thinking about Aunt Ida always filled her with dread. Where in the world did she run off to like that? And why? Who the hell was after her? Had they caught up to her yet?

The longing and despair, the laying down and trying to die from it all was—she knew, even in her young years—useless, futile, tiresome. The only thing shoulda-woulda-coulda ever got anybody was grief.

On that day she'd reluctantly returned home after wandering the streets aimlessly and accepted she would probably never get another job opportunity like that again. From then on, she got herself on up every day no matter how tired and uninspired she was. Shit. She still had to eat. And she still had people, family, to feed. She still had to survive.

Seemed to her all she was capable of doing was simply survivin'. All thoughts of love, fulfillment, dreams, and aspirations had to go away since it seemed survival was all she was set out to do. After all, all dreaming got a girl was heartache, disappointment, depression, and despair. If you let it take over, you'd look up and find the time passing by and you just sitting there looking stupid, feeling like a damn fool. She refused to do it. To be a fool. She decided to be smart. Practical. She would no longer lead a life laden with decisions based on emotions, whims, or whatever. From then on, she'd make decimated decisions, calculated choices. From then on, she'd simply survive.

It was the thing she'd always been good at, this survival. Even as a little girl. Even when she and Percy came up from North Carolina all alone, not knowing nothing about no New York except their momma was there. Yes, siree. Them two kids were scared as chickens before suppertime. All of the people. And all of the noise. When they stepped off that bus, all they had was each other and the instructions given to them:

'Don't go nowhere with nobody except your momma. Don't talk to no strangers. Don't look none of them crackers in the eye. And y'all two stick together.'

And that's what they did, she and Percy, they stuck together and figured out the citified place, which was so different from the country where they grew up. The trees that were here were stuck in concrete; the ones in the country came straight from dirt, grass, God's good earth. And here, all the kids had shoes on their feet. All of 'em. Even the coloured ones. And everything and everybody moved real fast and talked real fast, too.

Took her a while to catch on to what people were saying with their New York accents, but she did after a while since she was such a quick study. She even helped Percy understand what people were talking about since he was a little slow to catch on to things anyhow. She would never have imagined that he would have betrayed her so by not supporting her, by wanting her to stay stuck right there with him. What had happened to his fearlessness, his courage, the strength he showed when he grabbed her little hand, pulled her onto that bus with his back as steady as a maple tree and found them some seats side by side in the back of the segregated bus, the two of them together for the long ride up North? Where did *that* Percy go? 'Cause this ole scaredy-cat ass that he had become was something else entirely. But that was alright. Marie was about to be something else, too.

Chapter Seven

Three months later, when her girlfriends from work and school started getting their acceptance letters for the government jobs, she tried not to be jealous. Marie hated jealous women. So when this one and that one who'd applied and was accepted to the job-readiness program—whose main headquarters were in Washington D.C. where most of 'em would be headin' off to—shared their good news with her, she smiled her congratulations through the terrible torment. She'd never let any of 'em know how disappointed she was that she was unable to apply. No siree.

Besides, she had her own news to share, even though, in her typical fashion, she didn't share shit. Only her mother and her best friend Missy knew: she was marrying Mr. Conner. He'd asked her way too soon, about two months into their dating. And even though in the beginning she was just trying to have fun and forget Benjamin, Bob was suddenly so serious she started to take the situation serious, too. Still, she wasn't sure what she should do with his proposal, so she asked her mother, who, of course, encouraged the marriage, even insisted upon it, reminding Marie that 'don't no grown man got time to be playing around with no young girl. At least he wanna marry ya before he start messing witcha and good for him.'

Her mother was right, and his proposal was right on time. So they were gonna go right on down to the courthouse in Borough

Hall that afternoon, and they were gonna to make it official. Her mother approved wholeheartedly since she figured that if Marie was going to do something with herself, it might as well be this: marry a respected successful mature man who hung on her every word and looked at her like she was the cat's meow. She'd be living in that house over there on Ashland Place where they could put down roots but still build and grow. Yeah, it was going to be all right. Let all her girlfriends run off to D.C. and Virginia and wherever else the government had set up headquarters—some were even in Florida!—she'd be right here, making a home, married, and maybe happy. She hoped she'd be happy. What else could she do but hope? For the best. For the future. For herself. For happiness? Ha! Whatever it was that she forgot to know. She forgot her dreams of frivolous freedom, of travel, of youthful independence. She was getting married, and it was a good thing, a great choice, a blessing, but still…

She thought of Benjamin often. Even on her wedding night, when she was done making love to her husband, she'd wondered what it would have been like with Benjamin. At first, she felt guilty. Robert deserved her loyalty and her devotion. Hadn't he taken care of her, put her up in a nice home, made sure she had all new nice things, linens and silverware and chinaware and such? He even took her shopping for new clothes and hats and shoes; he wanted Marie to be put together whenever they went on the town. He'd lucked out and snagged himself a pretty young wife and he had every intention of showing her off. So when thoughts of Benjamin came into her mind, especially when her own husband was kissing or touching her, she felt right shameful.

But she soon noticed how he tipped his hat real slow at attractive women in the street and straight up smiled up in any woman's face—the coat check girl, the cigarette girl, the waitress—every chance he got. So she decided not to be guilty about any of that anymore. She realized that marriage made her married, but she was still Marie. She had lived and loved before her husband took her hand, and although she had no intention of being disloyal, she kept her thoughts of Benjamin near, like a personal purse of treasures tucked in her bosom that she could pull out, open up, look at, marvel over, and put right on back, away, where nobody knew it was there except her. She figured she deserved at least that.

After a while, she'd gotten into the swing of the marriage thing. Robert's daughter Frannie was sweet as pie but hesitant to really open up to the situation. But overall, it was easy. Marie knew how to take care of kids, having practically raised her mother's own. She knew the child, like all children, just needed to be accepted, to feel secure, to feel at home. Marie suspected the baby girl, who was only five years old at the time, was confused about the new living situation—she had to be!—so when Frannie asked:

'Miss Marie, what should I call you now?'

Marie told her point-blank:

'Call me Mamma, baby. From now on, I'm your mamma.'

That stepchild shit didn't sit well with Marie, and as far as she could tell from Frannie's relaxed relief as a response, the little girl didn't want to be considered anybody's step anything, either.

As for Frannie's own mother, Marie never knew the woman. Robert didn't talk much about it, so she figured she would just have to go on and keep speculating about the situation. The rumours were that the woman had died at childbirth. Some people said it maybe was a good thing since Robert had no intention of marrying her, and so she was sure to be shamed in the neighbourhood, although the poor woman wouldn't be the first to have a baby out of wedlock and sure 'nuff wouldn't be the last.

People said a lot of things: that she'd thrown herself at him hoping for marriage but got pregnant instead. Marie had also heard he refused to marry his daughter's mother because she had a reputation and therefore wasn't fit to marry, although clearly, she was good enough to hit the sheets with. There were also whisperings that he didn't want her because she was too dark—which is where Frannie got her beautiful mahogany skin colour, a colour that reminded Marie of Benjamin and made her cherish the child even more. She hoped Robert wasn't colour struck like her mother and that the latter was not true; she hoped none of it was true, honestly. But seeing that her husband cut the conversation short anytime she brought up the subject, she left it alone. She just didn't know and it was looking like she never would.

One thing she knew was that although she wasn't Frannie's mother, she was the next best thing. Marie made it her business to take good care of that precious child: dressed her up, pressed and curled her long thick hair, ironed her clothes, prepared her sandwiches, and made sure she felt right and loved at all times. It made her husband happy that the child had taken to Marie so smoothly, but it wasn't for him who she did it for, it was for that there Frannie, just as sweet and smart as she could be. It was nice to have a little girl around after being in her mother's house with all those bad boys all of the damn time. She did miss them sometimes, though, and her mother too. Some days, she would go on over to the old apartment and pay them a visit.

She never stayed too long, proclaiming that she had to get back to her housework and her husband, but really she found the over-crowded situation with her siblings suddenly claustrophobic. Still, she stopped in over there when she could and never went empty-handed, always picking up some lunch meat and bread from the corner deli for sandwiches for the boys and was always sure to bring a few of them big dill pickles her momma loved to munch on, loudly, one after the other. Sometimes she'd get over there and find herself tidying up like she used to, wiping down the sink, scrubbing the tub and such. And on days when not one of her brothers got around to sweeping those steps, she went on ahead and did that, too. The work assuaged the guilt she felt for leaving her mother and all of them right there in that old apartment for a new life, a new beginning, but mainly she felt the need to do it because when she married, she was still mad at her mother and secretly swore she'd never step foot in that old apartment again. It had worked for a while and the only time she would see her mother was when Harriett would visit Marie on the days she got out of the house to pay a bill or do a little shopping downtown. But then it got cold, and her mother didn't get out as much.

So Marie forgot to be mad and took herself on over there from time to time, putting all animosities aside. Sometimes instead of just stuff for sandwiches she'd pick up groceries—a whole chicken, greens, some flour for biscuits—and make a meal right there in her mother's little kitchen like she used to do. She found she missed this kind of cooking, although she never did it much in her own home just yet.

She'd told her husband she wasn't much of a cook and would open up a can of soup and serve it with a grilled cheese sandwich on the side for dinner for him and Frannie, and they ate it happily, and that was that. Oh, she made oatmeal for the baby girl and fried Robert's eggs in the morning—sizzling sunny side up the way he liked 'em. And each and every workday morning she brewed a fresh pot of hand ground coffee for the man. Toast and butter were easy enough, too. She kept things simple in her new kitchen as long as she could, never letting on that she was indeed quite a cook thanks to her mother and had surely learned a few things while working at Ida's. She'd spent half her life cooking big ole meals for hungry males, and she didn't feel like doing it no more, not just yet. So she made sure she burned a few pots to let her husband think she didn't know her way around a kitchen and the old fool believed her.

One day, though, she had a strong craving for white rice with red eye gravy. Just like that, outta nowhere, she had to have it. So she took the rice and put it on the stove to boil and then started chopping onions and stirring butter and flour in a pan to make her gravy. She'd already fried up a slab of bacon and removed it, leaving behind that good grease that was gonna make her gravy taste just right. There she was stirring and humming, all happy as hell, and in walks her husband hours before she expected him, hours before he usually got home. She had thought she was safe, that she could cook herself a savoury something then sit on down and enjoy it all alone before he brought his ass home from work in the evening. She figured she even had time to destroy the evidence by cleaning her pots real good with baking soda and a bit of bleach. But there he was, smack dab in the middle of the day, smiling at her and saying:

'Mmmm Marie. Something sure smells good in here...'

'Yeah, just making myself a lil' lunch,' she told him. 'Just some rice with gravy...'

'Well, woman, why you don't ever make me nothing good like that?' he demanded with a wink and a smile. She stared at him for a few seconds, blinked a couple times, sighed, sucked her teeth, then sent him off to the store with a good long grocery list. By the time he got home with a fresh cut chicken from the butcher shop, more flour and butter, some green beans, corn on the cob, heavy cream, chocolate powder, sugar, and eggs, she'd sat down and enjoyed her afternoon meal alone at the table as she'd intended.

When he got back, she got on up and into the kitchen and made her husband his first real home-cooked meal: fried chicken, sautéed green beans, creamed corn, biscuits, and some of her red eyed gravy. She even went on ahead and made the man a chocolate cake. He enjoyed it all, which sure enough made her smile, but she soon regretted letting him know what a good cook she was because it seemed like every couple of days he was calling home asking what's for dinner. He even started making requests like smothered pork chops or pot roast with potatoes. Once she started cooking, Bob couldn't get enough. Before long, he was bringing his work buddies home for dinner, talking loud to anyone who would listen about how his wife made the best brisket in Brooklyn. Every time she got annoyed with him and wanted to tell the nigga to make himself a sandwich and leave her the hell alone, she reminded herself that this man was her husband and she was his wife, so she went on ahead and made his meals.

What in the world was a wife anyway, she wondered. What a weighty word. What did it mean, really? Did it mean she was totally trapped or that she was instead instantly free? Blessed with the stability of a strong husband, the comfort and peace of mind of a stable home? Or burdened by the realization that this would be her life, this man, this place, that this was it. That there would be no dreams fulfilled or adventures experienced.

Later as an older woman, once her kids were grown, she would travel with her friends and sister Amy on cruises to Aruba and Bermuda and the like, and it was always amazing. Bus rides, boat trips, Marie was always eager to go, to get on out there, to travel, to see something. But at this point, while scrubbing pots and polishing silverware, she somehow knew she hadn't really done nothin' yet, that she hadn't really lived, hadn't seen none of the world. This was her world, right there in that house with her husband and daughter. She was grateful for it, make no mistake. People were starving all over, just hungry (and she herself would never forget being hungry as a girl as long as she lived). There was still a stupid war going on over there in Europe. So she knew better than to entertain thoughts of discontentment, of longing, of pitiful pipe dreams. She was practical. She was smart. So she kept her heart and mind firmly planted in gratitude and would go on to be blessed for it. She would have her own children eventually, and her husband would move her into a new home over there on President Street—a mini mansion—where Black doctors and dentists and rich Jews lived. She would never starve another day in her life, and her children would never know the pangs of hunger or the pain of poverty, and that would always, for Marie, be a source of pride.

Chapter Eight

It was her own mother who told her she'd be having a baby. Undeniably, Marie had put on some weight and even noticed herself that it was a little more challenging to button her blouses or zip-up her skirts lately. She'd figured with all that cooking—and eating—she was doing these days it was to be expected. She even made a mental note to cut back a bit; she didn't want to get too big and fat. She had to admit she liked being thicker like this, though. There was something soothing about being a bit round and always feeling full. After being hungry as a lion in winter when she was a little girl—when she could see her own ribs sticking out from her hand-me-down clothes—she sure wasn't gonna waste much time worrying herself about gaining some weight. But when Harriett saw her daughter that decisive day Marie was shocked and silent when the woman said right out:

'Marie. You pregnant.'

She hadn't been by her momma's house in a few weeks because once she started really cooking for her husband her work at home had more than doubled. Whoever said housework ain't real work is a damn liar. All that grocery shopping, cutting, chopping, mixing, frying, boiling, and baking, then serving it with a smile and cleaning it all up after. It was a lot if she had to say so herself. Marie didn't complain, though, as it gave her something to do during the day since Bob had insisted she stop working at the hospital once they got married. She thought it was a silly idea, especially that now she'd be living in the house on Ashland, closer to the hospital. She could get there on time for sure and even get in some overtime hours, being that getting home after dark would be a breeze since she was living right up the block. Besides, she knew a few of the girls at the job that had gotten married—some to local men, most to soldiers before they were sent off to the war like she and Benjamin was supposed to— and kept right on ahead working, even if their husbands had decent jobs or they was getting a check from the government for families of servicemen. But her husband wanted her home with Frannie, and she sure couldn't blame him for that. The girl needed some consistency, someone regular to rely on, to love. He made a good living down there at the Brooklyn Navy Yard, and, in addition to owning the home at Ashland, he had his hands in some other real estate situa- tions. So, far as Bob was concerned, they were doing just fine, good enough that no wife of his had to work outside of the home. So she finally agreed to give up her job at the hospital. What the hell? If the damn fool wanted to work and take care of her while she fussed about around the house all day cooking and cleaning, then let him go right on ahead and do it.

But Marie wasn't ready for nobody's baby, especially not her own. Which is why when her mother said what she said, she shrugged it off. She wasn't pregnant; it was just her mother's wishful thinking, Marie told herself over and over, hoping that her positive thoughts would make them true. That woman had wanted her to have babies ever since she married the man, even though she, of all people, had to know that the last thing Marie wanted to do was boil bottles, wipe-up spit up, scrub baby clothes on the washboard, and change dirty diapers.

'Why would you say something like that, Momma?' Marie demanded.

'Well, 'cause, girl, you got that glow. Nice and plump. Look at your hips and, mmm-hmm, you getting a lil' double chin…'

'Ain't a newly married woman supposed to gain some weight? Means she's happy and healthy and all that jazz?'

'Well, I wouldn't know nothing about that,' her never-married mother reminded her, turning to look her daughter square in her full face. 'But I do know a pregnant woman when I see one.'

Marie left Harriett's house shaking her head and saying Shit. Shit. Shit. The rest of the day was shit, and she said so over and over, out loud and under her breath. No matter what she was doing, she found herself thinking or saying or feeling like shit. She'd be bringing the mail from the mailbox and would just stop and say it:

Shit.

She'd be sweeping the floor in the foyer and would just stop and say it:

Shit.

She hadn't been to the doctor's yet to get her exam, to know for sure, but she knew she was pregnant and shit. Her mother's conviction was contagious, and as she replayed in her mind the times, late at night, when her husband would come to bed after a long hard day and start rubbing on her while she lay there all warm and soft under them fluffy blankets, she couldn't help but say it again, aloud:

Shit!

'What you over there shitting about, gal?' Robert asked, amused. She was in the kitchen fixing his dinner and must've forgotten he was there; she looked at him, startled, as if he was a stranger.

'Nothing, man,' she responded quickly. 'I just burned my finger on this stupid pot.'

'Aww,' he said and took her hand in his. He turned her palm over in his, and she let him. But when he tried to kiss the finger of her feigned burn, she pulled abruptly away. She didn't want him touching her just then. He'd done enough of that already, and look at what it got her. Pregnant. Shit.

Chapter Nine

That same night after visiting her mother, Marie made sure she was snoring hard and loud when her husband brought himself to bed, although she wasn't nowhere near asleep. She couldn't rest. She was too busy praying, crying silently inside, and begging the Lord or whoever was listening to make it not be true.

But of course, it was true, and the next week the doctor confirmed it. He was nonchalant when he told her to take good care of herself, get her rest, gave her some big orange vitamins to try to swallow, and sent her on her way. Which way? She didn't know. She was lost. She was still figuring out how to be a wife and some kind of mother to a lonely little girl and now here she was about to have her very own baby. Lord Have Mercy.

Seems soon as she left the doctor's office, she got really tired. Exhausted. All she wanted to do was sleep. The doctor and her momma warned her to expect as much, but this was different. It wasn't like she was physically tired. She was young and still had all the strength and energy in the world, pregnant or not. It was more like that emotional exhaustion again. She couldn't explain it. Looking at the life she'd chosen and realizing she had no choice now—she'd have to live it, that there was no going back, that this was it—made her so weary she could weep. Did anyone ever get the lives they really wanted, she wondered?

On her way home from the doctor that very day, she saw a girl on roller skates whiz past her, and she burst into tears thinking of her roller derby days. She figured she was being emotional and hormonal, but that wasn't it. It was this: she'd been a badass roller-skater! When it came to competitive roller-skating, she'd been darn good, especially at them derbys. She'd strap on her skates and her kneepads and her hard as hell helmet and set out across that roller rink, and none of them guinea or ghetto girls could catch her. Yeah, she'd been bumped and bruised and she sure enough, went tumbling tough more than a few times. But she'd always jump right back up, nimble as a cat, and get back into the game. Soon enough, she had to stop that, too. Too dangerous, her mother and brother said. It was for wild girls, Harriett had informed her along with Percy, who insisted Marie always act like a lady, whatever that meant.

She scoffed to herself as she watched the skating girl in the street until she was out of her eyesight. Morosely, Marie realized she was envious of the child who'd looked so free, so happy, who had to be about eleven years old, a good age for a girl, fearless and just having fun, not developed yet so not self-conscious about their bodies, no bras digging into their back, no girdles gripping into 'em, no sanitary belts slowing 'em down.

At that moment, Marie realized she had never really been free, and now it was looking like she never would be. The open window of the young woman she used to be was closing. Now with this baby growing in her womb, she had no doubt that she was irrevocably grown. She now would have a person to guide, to protect, to teach, to nurture, which was overwhelming, especially when all she wanted to do was to protect, guide, and nurture herself. But that's what mothers did, didn't they? They made compromises and sacrifices for the sake of their children. They had to. They're the ones who'd laid down and pushed the things out into this wild world. But why? Was it ever worth it? Marie mused.

And why now? That's what she really wanted to know. Especially when there was a war going on. There were fools out there killing Jews in Germany and lynching Negroes down south. What kind of world would she be bringing a child into? What in the world was she doing? She could feel it. The fear forming. Fear for what her unborn child would ultimately face in this cold, cruel world. Fear that came from having the blood of slaves running through her very veins. Fear that she would somehow teach her own children what she herself had been taught: how to submit and survive simultaneously. Fear that no matter how hard she would try or whatever she could possibly do she could never really protect her children from bigots, bullets, bullshit. She took a deep breath in a feeble attempt to pull herself together. She had to get the house ready for when Bob came home from work. But first, she had to take a nap.

When Marie woke up she was surprised to hear conversation coming from the dining room downstairs. She strained her ears, but she could only make out a few muffled voices. She sure hoped her husband hadn't brought none of his friends or business people home with him that evening looking for her to cook and serve and smile and shit; Marie was not in the mood. Nevertheless, she straightened herself up, freshened up in the bathroom with a warm washcloth, added a spritz of perfume, put on a little lipstick, and went on downstairs, dreading every step she took, even pausing a few times to stop and stand and sigh and still, after a nice nap, say 'shit!'

'There she is! There's my beautiful wife,' Robert announced the moment her foot hit the last step where he could see her from the dining room. She did not feel beautiful, did not want to smile, and so she wanted to shake him right on out of his ridiculously merry mood. She noticed the case where he kept his liquor was ajar and that he held a half full highball glass in his hand.

'*Oh*,' she thought. 'He's drunk. That's why he's so happy.' But she didn't begrudge him his buzz since he was thankfully not a heavy drinker. Not like his sister, who loved her gin. Mercifully Maime hadn't moved in with them yet. But it was only a matter of time, and Marie knew it. She didn't even know Bob had a sister until she'd married the man since Maime was a creature of the night, as some would say. But not in a bad way. She actually worked at the hospital, too, but was on the night shift. For the most part, she slept during the day most times at her long-time boyfriend's room up the block until the both of 'em, drunk as skunks and late with lodging fees, decided Bob's house was a better place for them to squat. But that was thankfully a later day.

This evening, her husband announced:

'We have company, honey!'

He stood slowly, smiling at her and slurring his words a little.

She took the few small footsteps from the hall to the living room, rounded the corner, and saw two people sitting there, relieved that it wasn't his sister or any of Bob's work buddies.

It was Missy and her new man. Marie was visibly pleased. Even though she wasn't in any mood for any company, she was glad it was her friend tonight and not one of her husband's. And it was good to see Missy, whom she hadn't laid eyes on since she moved out of the room upstairs into her own little place down on Myrtle and Vanderbilt. It had been weird not seeing Missy every day, catching up during their shifts at the hospital. But eventually, with all Marie had going on, she got used to it. That evening, though, her friend sure was a sight for sore eyes standing there dressed to the nines in a green outfit she made on her own, 'the hell with those expensive, racist department stores,' she'd said, with gloves and a little pill hat and a purse to match. Yeah, her girl was looking good with her bad self.

'Hey, Marie, how you been?' Missy came right over to her and gave her a warm hug. It felt good to see her old friend and Marie found herself relaxing a bit in her brief embrace.

'This here, Mr. Oliver,' Missy announced, answering Marie's

question before she could even ask it. Marie smiled at the handsome man and extended her hand, which he grabbed gregariously when he stood to greet her. 'Well, at least he's a gentleman,' Marie thought to herself.

'So nice to finally meet you,' Mr. Oliver said in a voice as deep as the Mississippi river.'Missy here talk about you all the time. We sure sorry to pop on over unannounced like this, but Missy made me promise to drive by here on our way to the picture show.'

'It's fine,' she said as she sat down to her husband's surprise. He was looking like he'd expected her to offer their guests something to eat or to refill their drinks, but when she didn't, he sat himself right back down at the table, too. He offered his wife a drink, but she declined. She didn't really like liquor anyway, and now that she was pregnant, she knew this wasn't the time to start messing with the stuff.

The four of them made small talk for a few minutes, most of which centred around the war and what all was going on. Any talk of the battles made her anxious and uncomfortable, and Missy knew this about her. Marie looked over at her friend and could tell she had something on her mind, too. Wasn't no way she was gonna just pop in uninvited unless she had something specific to say.

So Marie excused herself from the table, told the gentlemen she was going into the kitchen to whip up something to eat and took her friend with her. Once they got into the kitchen, Missy got right to the point.

'I was working at the hospital yesterday in the intensive care unit and heard somebody calling me real low, in a whisper like. I looked over to see, and it was Ms. Miller. Benjamin's momma.'

'What was she doing in the hospital? She alright?' Marie asked while busying herself with pots and pans. She was just going to heat up some chicken she'd made yesterday and serve it with a little rice and salad. It was the best she could pull together at such short notice.

She had meant to make a proper meal—her husband did work hard all day, after all, and it was the least she could do—but her nap had lasted longer than she'd intended.

'Yeah, she alright, I guess. She went home today, but she was there for her pressure. The doctor said it was so high she damn near had a stroke. Sent her off with some pressure pills and told her to rest herself some.'

'Well, what did she want with you?' Marie whispered.

'That's the thing. She didn't want to talk to me at all. She knows we friends, and she wants to talk with you. Told me to tell you to come see her soon as you can.'

Marie stopped.

'Did she say anything about Benjamin? How he holding up over there?' Even though her husband was right in the next room, Marie couldn't stop herself from needing to know.

'I asked her. You know I did. And she just waved me away. She says she only wants to talk to you.'

'Well, what in the world she wants with me?'

'I don't know, girl. Like I said. She just wants you to come see her soon as you can.'

'Well, I suppose I can go tomorrow, but…'

'Go ahead, Marie. I'll come over and watch Frannie for a few hours if that's what you worrying about,' Missy said, reading her friend's mind.

Marie nodded yes and said nothing else since she didn't want her husband to hear them there in the kitchen. He didn't know nothing about 'ole Benjamin or his proposal or his momma or her broken heart, and Marie wanted to keep it that way, so she stopped talking. She completely shut off and even forgot to tell her friend the news that she was going to have a baby. That would have to wait. Besides, she knew once she said it out loud to anyone, it would really be real, and she wasn't quite yet ready for her new reality.

For the rest of the evening, she fretted. She didn't hardly get any sleep that night, either. She knew something was wrong, that something had happened to Benjamin. She just knew it in her gut. What else would his mother want with her?

The next morning after she got Robert out the door and Missy showed up as promised, Marie took her hat, purse, and gloves and headed on over to Ms. Miller's house, her heart in her mouth the whole time.

When she got to the apartment, Benjamin's mother, who was as dark and slim and lanky as her son, confirmed Marie's deepest fears and most constant worry: her Benjamin had been killed overseas. His mother didn't know how and surely didn't know why and neither did Marie. All Ms. Miller knew was what the soldier man said when he came to her door three days before, sending her blood pressure so high that she had to go to the hospital. Marie stood there in shock and could not speak until Benjamin's mother spoke for her:

'Marie, I know you gotta know he loved you, baby. Was so hurt when your momma said he couldn't marry you. I had a mind to go over there and speak to her myself, tell her what a fine girl you are, how y'all would make a happy couple with beautiful babies. But... you know I prayed on it and left it alone. You can't change people's minds about some things no matter how hard you try. Some people just got their own way of seeing things...'

'He shouldn't have listened to her,' Marie interrupted, then corrected herself. '*We* shouldn't have listened to her. So what, he didn't have no fancy job, and we would be living in the same neighbourhood. So what he couldn't do nothin' for me just yet? We shoulda ignored her, proved her wrong about him...'

Ms. Miller put down the teacup she had been sipping from and leaned forward in her seat.

'Is that what he told you your momma said? Hmph...'

'Yes, ma'am. And you know, momma means well. She just wants

me to be happy and all, and she knew we were young, me and Benjamin…'

Frustrated, irritated, and in a pain that can only come to a woman who has lost her only son, Ms. Miller spoke with a callousness that cut Marie to the bone, as was her intention.

'Your mother, that Harriet, she told my boy he was too black for you. Did you know that? Do you hear me, girl? Too black. Dark as dirt. She didn't want y'all making no black babies out here, that's what she said. That's what she told him, straight to his face. Ole ignorant heifer. Said a boy black as Benny could never get nowhere. Shit. She's worse than a white woman, that mother of yours…'

At first, Marie wanted to interject, was going to protest, to defend her mother. But the more Ms. Miller spoke, the more Marie knew what she said was true. She knew how her mother felt about dark-skinned black folks and how superior she felt because of her cream-coloured complexion. She remembered her mother scolding Marie, always telling her to stay out of the sun, and how when she and Percy first came up North, she commented on how dark they were and how she didn't sound happy about it. Then there were the men. Marie suddenly saw the faces of the men that her mother entertained. Some were nice men, gentlemanly and generous. Some—most—were full of shit. All, though, were fair-skinned. Or, as the kids would tease her, 'light, bright and almost white.' Marie hated those taunts, hated being called 'high yeller' or even 'yeller gal'. Some people even offered it up as a compliment. She never understood it. After what she'd seen down there in North Carolina, how ugly and disgusting and mean most whites were towards coloured folks—whether you were light or dark, they didn't care. To them, you were black and they treated you just like that. Just like dirt. So why did people, her people, her mother, want to look like them? Damn fools. This world sometimes…

'My mother ain't got no sense…' Marie said softly. She didn't know what else to say.

'Well…' Ms. Miller, seeing Marie's discomfort and despair, eased up. 'It's all water under the bridge now. You'd be a widow today anyway.'

Ms. Miller turned away from Marie to face the small window in the cramped apartment, the window that faced a brick wall. It was the truth, and Marie knew it, and worse, she felt it. If they woulda went ahead and got married, she'd be sitting here a war widow. Strangely she felt like one anyway. No, they had never been married, and yes, she'd married another, but she was devastated just the same. She felt like an idiot, too, for listening to her mother, for listening to him, for not fighting for their love. Isn't that what she did best? Fight? Everything she ever had she had to fight for—even a scrap of food—yet she didn't fight for him, for them.

Benjamin's mother walked away from the window and passed Marie, stopping to stand next to a small dresser near the bed. It was the bed where Benjamin had proposed, where they kissed. Where they did not make love. Marie was nauseous now. The memories coming back to her were making her woozy and full of regret. She shoulda let him have her. Hell. *She* shoulda had *him*. She'd wanted him to touch her everywhere, but she made him stop. What a shame. What a waste. She shoulda went on ahead and did what the hell she wanted to do without paying nobody no never mind. Maybe then she might be sitting here with *his* baby inside of her instead of sitting here feeling like a fool, empty. She'd have herself a little piece of him. She'd be able to look into eyes that looked like his, hear his laugh, maybe see his smile when the baby smiled. But this here wasn't Benjamin's baby. It was hers. And her husband's. And that was that.

She stood up to leave but her feet could barely move. She was dizzy. Sweating slightly, she asked Ms. Miller for a glass of water and the woman politely obliged. She accepted the water graciously but not without guilt. Wasn't Marie the one that was supposed to be serving her, helping her, asking her if she needed anything? The poor woman. Benjamin was all she had, and now she had no one. Marie had her husband, little Frannie, all her brothers, her sister Amy and yes, her mother. She wasn't alone in this world, and this realization strengthened her somehow. She knew she'd soon fall apart, though. She knew what Ms. Miller had told her about her love, her sweet love, had not quite hit her yet. But she knew it was coming. She had to go.

'Wait a minute, baby,' Ms. Miller said, fumbling around with a mess of papers and envelopes there on her dresser.

'He wanted you to have this.'

Ms. Miller pushed the papers into Marie's hands. She stared in disbelief.

'He said if anything happened to him over there, he wanted you to have something, for you to be taken care of. I guess he didn't know you'd be married, but I'm not gonna pay that no mind. That doesn't matter. This is what he wanted, so this is what it is.'

Marie looked down and saw that these were his pension checks his mother had set aside for her. She had so many questions, but there was no Benjamin, so there were no answers. He was dead, and she was going to have to live with that. But she could not accept the money. She was not his wife and was not entitled to it. More so, his mother never had to tell her about it in the first place. She could have kept it all to herself. But she did not. She actually honoured her son's last wishes. Marie was moved to tears. Through watery, burning eyes, she placed the envelopes back into the feeble woman's hands and got on out of there while she could still stand.

Dinner that evening was a disaster. She tried to make biscuits but her hands let the bag of flour simply slip onto the floor; there was flour dust everywhere even after she swept up. She'd have to get a wet mop on that soon. While she was sweeping, she forgot the green beans in the pot on the back of the stove, so they burned at the bottom. And although she was quick enough to pull the non-burnt ones out of the pot and put them in a dish so they could be somewhat edible, the house now held the smell of burned vegetables, which Marie hated. So she opened herself a window and went on back to making her meal. But she couldn't do anything right at all. Everything she did failed. She cut herself when she was chopping a cucumber for the salad she'd settled on fixing since she knew she couldn't burn that. When she reached for the dish towel to press against the blood coming from her forefinger, her elbow knocked her favourite glass bowl off of the counter and onto the floor. It thankfully did not shatter. It just broke into five large pieces. She stared down at them, trying to figure out if she could use some of that good industrial glue to put the beautiful bowl back together, if she could somehow salvage it. But Marie could see that she could not. Some things, once broken, could never be fixed.

When Bob came home, he found her standing in the kitchen staring at the broken bowl on the floor. She was sobbing softly. He, of course, wanted to know what was wrong with her; he'd never seen her so distraught, disorganized, distracted. She hadn't even fed Frannie yet, who was just fine playing quietly with her dolls and blocks. But Bob was still taken aback by Marie's mood. He wondered if he should slap her hard across the face to snap her out of this scary state but thought better of it, remembering the fight they got into earlier on in their marriage when she'd made him so angry that he'd lifted his hand to her. Before he could land a blow, she'd grabbed a broom and held it in front of her like shield and sword and said:

'Nigga you go on ahead and try it and one of us is dying up in here tonight, and you best believe it ain't gonna to be me.'

No. That was no way to deal with this woman. Whatever was wrong with her, he didn't know, so he just waited and watched her until she said slowly:

'I'm sorry about dinner...'

'Aww, Marie, don't worry about that it's all right as long as you all right.' He felt helpless and confused by his wife's strange disposition. 'Just tell me what's wrong wit 'cha, that's all. What's the matter?'

Well, what could she say? What could she tell him? Why even bother? His ego would surely be hurt by seeing her sob over some man other than him, over someone he didn't even know ever existed. No he would never understand. So she decided he didn't deserve to know. This was her loss, her pain that cut so deep it made her selfish. It was her very own beastly burden that she did not care to share. So she spoke her other truth and told her husband what the doctor had said: she was going to have a baby.

Her husband laughed, relieved.

'Aww, girl, that ain't nothing to be carrying on up in here about. That's good news. You in here looking like somebody done died.'

Marie shuddered at these words, but he did not notice. Pleased and excited at the baby news, he kept right on talking.

'A baby is a good thing, Marie. I know you scared, but it's gonna be all right, you'll see. C'mon,' he reached out to her, grabbed ahold of her shoulders and pulled her into his chest. She was numb and in shock, and so she let him hold her.

'Let's go out tonight. The three of us. Let's grab a bite to eat. Anywhere you want to go. Besides, this kitchen looks like it's had enough action for one day,' he said, laughing lightly into her neck, his eyes surveying the cluttered countertop, open cabinets, burned pot, broken bowl, and flour-dusted floor.

With her head burrowed in his shoulder, he could not see her tears. They were the silent ones, thankfully, and she did not sob. She had done that already—in the hallway after stepping out of Ms. Millers' apartment, on the street walking to catch the bus, on the ride all the way home. Right there on public transportation she'd turned her wet face towards the window while she wept, wilfully ignoring concerned stares from perfect strangers. She made it home, bleary-eyed and puffy-faced, and then fell apart again in the living room as Missy looked on in helpless horror. What was wrong? What happened? Was there anything she could do? In broken-hearted babble, she told her friend the worst had happened; what they had suspected was indeed true. He was gone. Dead. Damn fool done got his self killed out there somewhere in Germany, so far away from home.

Now, here she was, letting her husband hold her until, warily, out of guilt, she backed away. She couldn't let him comfort her, not through this.

The loss of her one true love would be the only secret she ever kept from her husband, and it wasn't even hard to hide. He worked every single weekday, went out on the weekends, and came on home whenever he wanted. He sure stayed busy and as their life progressed and their family grew and his responsibilities mounted turned out he wasn't that in tune with her anyhow. Still, she was grateful for him. He was smart and innovative and educated and ambitious and a good provider. But he wasn't Benjamin and he never would be. This realization saddened yet satiated her during her long hard first pregnancy and then throughout them all.

Each child she bore for Bob made her more his woman, each child she pushed out pulled her away from her past and planted her firmly in her present; he gave her good reason to stay busy, to keep occupied, distracted. The love for Benjamin she poured into them, feeding them, loving them, spoiling them, caring for them so that they didn't have to ever pick up a broom as often as she did when she was a girl. She kept herself occupied by giving them a privileged childhood, catering to them, and being there always for her children and her husband. All this so she would not dwell on her forever love, dead and gone like all her girlish dreams, although, of course, some things a woman just doesn't ever forget, distractions be dammed.

She didn't want to go out to dinner that night, although it would have been nice. She *was* already dressed. She would only have to remove her apron, fix her face, and grab her purse. Nevertheless, she realized that where she wanted to be, at that moment, was where she stood. In her home. In her kitchen. She told him this and thankfully he didn't protest. Instead he left her alone to go wash off his workday, leaving her standing in the same spot he found her. She said a silent prayer to the good Lord to just get her through this day, the day she found out about Benjamin's death. If he gave her the strength to do that, just tolerate this terrible day, she knew she could surely face the others that lay before her.

Of course, she couldn't know what was to come. The children she would have. The children and grandchildren she would bury. The traveling she would do. The laughter she'd experience. The pain. The influence she would have on her daughters, granddaughters, and great-granddaughters, in the way they carried themselves, spoke, thought, and lived just by her being present, just by being in their lives. She'd no way of knowing she'd die there, right in that kitchen, recently remodelled; that she would live to see the first Black president elected to the White House and watch him sit there, shining, for four good years. She couldn't know that, after walking on up to the Brooklyn Technical High School (where four of her grandchildren would graduate) around the corner with her oldest and youngest daughter to vote Obama in for a second term, she would come home here, make a little something to eat, sit down at her kitchen table, the same table where she'd served her husband his first real meal, where she'd made Easter, Thanksgiving and Christmas dinners for her family for years and years and years, and die, without warning, right there. Just like that. She wouldn't experience any physical pain or failing bodily functions. No, there were no bad knees, hip surgeries, cataracts, or persistent pressure pills in her future. She would live healthy, sharp-minded, and capable until she was ninety-one years old. She would be here one day and the next she'd be simply gone. She didn't know any of that.

All she knew right then was that suddenly, out of nowhere, music filled the house. Robert must have turned the radio on in the hallway on his way upstairs. At first she was annoyed. She really wanted, even needed, silence. But Count Basie's 'Boo Hoo', with its upbeat rhythm and sad lyrics saying, 'boo hoo, you got me crying for you, and as I sit here and sigh oh my, I can't believe it's true…' was blaring through the hallway all the way into her kitchen.

In order to make the music stop Marie would have to go on up there and ask Bob to turn it off, or down, or at least change the station altogether. But she didn't bother. She knew it was one of his favourite tunes and even surprisingly smiled to herself thinking of him humming it that first night in Harlem. So, instead of going into the hallway and turning

the damn radio off her own self, she simply listened to the music and moved to the melody, one note at a time.

THE END

About the Author

Errol Fyfe/Hellen Collen Imaging

Kerika Fields is a New York-based writer and photographer whose work has been published and exhibited widely. Her articles have appeared in *Essence*, *Variety*, *VIBE*, and *The Source*, among others. She is also the author of *He's Gone… You're Back: The Right Way to Get Over Mr. Wrong* (Kensington Publishing). *With Your Bad Self* is her first book with Jacaranda Books. She currently lives in Brooklyn with her daughter, husband, and cat Smokey.

Visit her at withyourbadself.com